Sister Agnes

The History of
King Edward VII's Hospital
for Officers
1899–1999

Some books by the same author

Captain James Cook
Mountbatten: Hero of Our Time
Edwina: Countess Mountbatten of Burma
Louis and Victoria: The First Mountbattens
Edward and Alexandra
Victoria and Albert
The Great War at Sea 1914–1918
Captain Bligh and Mr Christian
The Fleet That Had to Die
Admirals in Collision

Sister Agnes

The History of
King Edward VII's Hospital
for Officers
1899–1999

RICHARD HOUGH

JOHN MURRAY
Albemarle Street, London

© Richard Hough 1998

First published in 1998
by John Murray (Publishers) Ltd,
50 Albemarle Street, London W1X 4BD

The moral right of the author has been asserted

A catalogue record for this book is available from the British Library

ISBN 0-7195-5561-2

Typeset in Monotype Bembo by Servis Filmsetting Ltd, Manchester
Printed and bound in Great Britain by the University Press, Cambridge

Contents

Contents

Illustrations

The author and publisher would like to thank the following for permission to reproduce illustrations: Plates 1, 5, 6, 7, 8, 15, 16, 17, 18, 19, 20, 21, 22, 23, 24, 25, 26, 27, 28, King Edward VII's Hospital archives; 2, 9, 10, 11, 12, 13, 14, Hulton Getty; 3, Weidenfeld & Nicolson; 4, The Director, National Army Museum, London.

Acknowledgements

I wish to acknowledge the gracious permission of the Queen for access to the Royal Archives at Windsor Castle.

Queen Elizabeth the Queen Mother kindly offered me her comments on the Hospital, which she has visited on a number of occasions.

The Duke of Kent, President of the Hospital, was generous with both his time and his thoughts.

I would also like to thank two past Matrons of the Hospital, Miss Margaret Dalglish MVO and Miss Dorothy Shipsey MVO, now Countess Cadogan, for their sharing of memories.

The late Sir Brian Warren and the late Vere, Lady Birdwood CVO were very helpful on the early days in Beaumont Street.

The following are among those many people who were kind enough to write, of their own accord or in answer to several appeals for facts and reminiscences of the Hospital's long life: Admiral of the Fleet Sir Henry Leach GCB DL; Brigadier C. J. M. Harrisson OBE; the late Sir Anthony Dawson KCVO MD FRCP; R. W. Lloyd-Davies MS FRCS; Rear Admiral Charles Weston CB, one-time Appeals Secretary; Mrs Margaret Pell; Commander M. B. St John RN; Major P. B. Hall; Colonel D. Smiley LVO OBE MC; Lady Butter; Brigadier E. G. B. Davies Scourfield; Mrs Christine Lucas; Rear Admiral G. A. Thring CB DSO DL; Air Commodore Charles Simpson CBE MA; Mrs Margaret Sperling; Miss Ann Keyser; Dame

Acknowledgements

Moura Lympany and Miss Margaret Strickland, joint authors of *Moura: Her Autobiography*; Brigadier B. T. V. Cowey DSO OBE DL; Mrs Peter West and Miss Sandra West.

I owe an incalculable debt to Air Vice-Marshal Alfred Beill CB, Appeals Secretary during the greater part of the time I spent writing this book; and to Caroline Cassels, who gave me an essential Matron's-eye view of the Hospital today, which was confirmed by my emergency two-week stay as a patient just as this book was going to press.

Introduction

SISTER AGNES KEYSER was a remarkable woman, born at the height of the Victorian era and living into the age of bombardment of open cities. 'This is my third war!' she exclaimed in a letter to a friend in 1939. Indeed, twentieth-century wars shaped her life. In the last days of the dying nineteenth century, she asked her friend the then Prince of Wales what she could do to help the country's war in South Africa. He suggested that she should turn her substantial house in Belgravia into a hospital for wounded officers.

She had no formal training – the title 'Sister' was bestowed on her by the Prince – but supported by some of the most notable medical consultants of the day and by hand-picked nursing staff, she was soon receiving casualties from the Boer War. Sister Agnes was a small, dashing, apparently tireless figure, who undertook her duties with the same loyalty and enthusiasm earlier demonstrated by Florence Nightingale. She was also a person of determined views, described by her sailor patients as 'running a tight ship'.

When peace was finally declared, the newly crowned King Edward VII, without much difficulty, persuaded Sister Agnes to keep her hospital open, naming it after himself. He also persuaded some of his rich friends to contribute to the running costs, which until then had been met by the considerable fortunes of Agnes and her sister, Fanny.

Since the royal opening of the permanent Hospital in 1904, every successive sovereign has acted as Patron, and a senior member of the Royal Family as President of what is formally King Edward VII's Hospital for Officers: Founder Sister Agnes.

PART I

Belgravia

CHAPTER I

The Keyser Origins

A LL THAT IS known about the early Keyser family is that they arrived in England in the eighteenth century from central Europe and, like many other Jews, set up in London as traders. It was an advantageous time to do so and they rapidly prospered. The first family member of whom there is any record was Alfred Keyser (pronounced 'Keeser'; from their earliest days they were particular about the name's correct pronunciation), born at the end of the eighteenth century and believed to be the second of the naturalized generation. In spite of the prolonged economic drain of the Napoleonic Wars, Alfred Keyser not only survived but did very well in the City of London. The Keysers' country house was Cross Oak, Great Berkhamsted, Hertfordshire. One imagines that Alfred was thankful when Robert Stephenson completed the London to Birmingham railway in 1837, greatly reducing the time taken to travel from Berkhamsted to Euston Square, and thence by a growler (four-wheeled cab) to the City.

Alfred Keyser married and had two sons, Frederic Charles and Arthur Louis. Frederic married Louisa Frances Marshall. Meanwhile, Alfred had decided to become a stockbroker, and was elected a member of the Stock Exchange in 1835. Over the following years, he developed a friendship and a close business association with Henry D. Ricardo, like himself one of a large immigrant family who had prospered. In 1857 they decided to collaborate in the stockbroking business as Keyser

& Ricardo, which rapidly went from strength to strength. At one time the collaboration was further strengthened by a marriage between the families. Both families had long since abandoned their Jewish faith, and all the children were baptized as Christians.

Another scion of the family, Charles Keyser, married Margaret Blore, and together they bought an estate between the villages of Stanmore and Bushey in Hertfordshire. They had one son, Charles Edward (born 1847) and three daughters, Frances (born 1850), Agnes (born 11 July 1852) and Marion (born 1854). The three girls were happy at Warren House, a magnificent place with rolling lawns scattered with wellingtonias, a large boating lake and formal gardens requiring the attention of a dozen gardeners.

The girls were educated privately but took part in the usual village activities. A surviving press cutting tells of Agnes singing in a concert at Stanmore: 'This lady has a fine, clear and flexible voice.' Agnes, though slight and frail looking, was the dominant one. Frances (always known as Fanny) worshipped her younger sister.

Charles was sent to Eton, the girls completed their studies at home and then the time came for Fanny to 'come out'. She had no desire to face her first season alone, and pleaded for Agnes to accompany her on the taxing round of balls and dinners, and the presentation at Court.

Their father, to whom money was no object, had bought a mansion in Chester Place, Hyde Park Square, and this was to be the girls' base for the season. Agnes relished the social activity.

Meanwhile, brother Charles had come down from Trinity, Cambridge, where he obtained his BA in 1873. He had inherited his father's business capacity, but also shone at cricket and captained the Hertfordshire County Cricket team for a number of years. He married Emma Mary Bagnall, and they decided to move out further from London. They did this in a very splendid, typical Keyser style by buying the entire village and lordship of Aldermaston in Berkshire. Like his father, Charles had three daughters and a son.

After their first season, Agnes and Fanny also left Warren House, in their case for fashionable Belgravia in London. The sisters were very close, yet very different in personality. Fanny was quiet and introspective and easily made shy; Agnes was extrovert, talkative and a great charmer. She loved social life and titled people, especially if they were amusing. Agnes was also the prettiest of the three sisters. Marion, the youngest, married early, after which little is known about her.

As Fanny and Agnes became established on the London scene, their father transferred a generous proportion of his investments to the two young women, and bought the leasehold of a large house for them near Hyde Park Corner, 17 Grosvenor Crescent. Here they entertained lavishly and over the years built up a wide circle of friends, all of them 'the best people'. At weekends or when social life in London ceased at the end of the season at Cowes, they would be invited to grand houses in England or Scotland. Neither showed any desire to marry.

On 27 February 1898 the Keyser sisters were invited to dine at the home of Colonel the Hon. George Keppel and his wife, Alice. It was not their first visit, and Agnes especially liked the Colonel, every inch a soldier and a son of the 7th Earl of Albemarle. His beautiful young wife was described as being 'known in Society for her vivacity and wit, her knowledge of what went on in the narrow but fascinating world in which she lived, and her equal capacity for recounting and listening to anecdotes. Well informed on people and events, she also possessed a nature which prohibited her from uttering an uncharitable word about anyone.'[1]

Agnes liked and approved of the Hon. Alice Keppel in every particular. But at that February dinner party there was someone else present for the first time, the Prince of Wales. Alice, as hostess, ensured that the heir to the throne sat on her right. Everyone present that evening, including the Keyser sisters, observed the effect the twenty-nine-year-old Alice had on the fifty-six-year-old Prince. He was clearly enchanted by her good looks and wit and cleverness. What the other guests were witnessing was the birth of a love that was to endure for the Prince's lifetime. The relationship was to be quite unlike the numerous affairs in which the Prince had become involved – with Sarah Bernhardt, the Countess of Warwick or Lillie Langtry, to name but three. These other affairs were mere dalliances, but Alice Keppel became the only lasting woman in his life, with the exception of his wife – and the role of Princess Alexandra had become, like her hearing, somewhat muted.

There was, however, one other woman at that dinner party whom the Prince of Wales noted and clearly approved of, although in quite a different way. When Agnes Keyser looked up at her future sovereign after her brisk curtsy, he noted a diminutive, pretty woman in her mid-forties, with trustworthy blue eyes and a friendly but by no means disrespectful expression on her face. The Prince had long ago acquired the capacity for slipping people he met into his mental card-index system where they were always available. The name Keyser also struck a chord. It was a City name, surely, associated with friends like Sir Ernest Cassel, the late Baron Maurice de Hirsch, Bischoffsheim and Goldschmidt: some of the City men who had served the Prince well in the management of his private finances. The Prince of Wales chatted with this little woman for a short time before taking his place at the table.

The dinner continued, course after course, the Prince leaving little on his plate. The Colonel and his wife were noted for their fine table, as Agnes had witnessed before.

Not long after that delightful and interesting evening, Agnes received a telephone call from someone speaking from 'the Prince of Wales's office'. The gentleman on the line spoke of the Prince's pleasure at meeting her and wondered if the Prince and their hostess of that evening, Alice Keppel, might call at 17 Grosvenor Crescent for tea one afternoon the following week. A mutually convenient day was agreed. Agnes had not reached the age of forty-five, living in society, without acquiring a sophisticated knowledge of the ways of the world, and she was flattered that after only one brief meeting the heir to the throne had trusted her discretion to such a degree. The day arrived, and one imagines Mrs Keppel's carriage was the first to arrive, the Prince of Wales anonymously in a growler, and without an equerry, a little later. One can be almost certain, too, that after a suitable interval, and the pouring of tea, the two guests were left alone.

The visits became increasingly frequent, and the Keyser sisters recognized that they were privy to and, indeed, encouraging the development of an intimate and deep relationship between the future King of England and this brilliant and beautiful younger woman.

Later, this relationship stabilized and was accepted widely, even by the Princess of Wales, who liked Alice Keppel better than some of her husband's earlier mistresses. Nor did Colonel Keppel take exception to the relationship. When the Prince succeeded to the throne as King Edward VII he was, as before, invited to most of the great houses of England and Scotland. Alice Keppel was invited, too – and with relief, for she kept him happy and there were few tantrums when she was around. One of his biographers has written:

> Alice Keppel was good-natured, humorous and discreet. She smoked cigarettes through a long holder, and spoke in a deep, throaty voice. Her zest for life was infectious and she was gay without being frivolous. Nobody had fewer enemies and there was nothing self-seeking about her. She loved the King for himself and understood his moods. Hence the skill with which she handled him. Once, when they were playing bridge together – and His Majesty was recognised to be more formidable as a partner than an opponent – he began to get angry with her for muddling her cards. She remained, however, unmoved, excusing herself on the grounds that she 'never could tell a King from a Knave'.[2]

In the same month as that dinner party in London, February 1898, there occurred an event six thousand miles away in South Africa that in a circuitous manner would be linked with it. The Boer leader, Paul Kruger, was re-elected President of Transvaal 'by a massive majority'. Troubles for England had been mounting in South Africa for some time. A foolhardy English South African, Starr Jameson, had secretly organized and then in early 1896 carried out a raid deep into the independent Transvaal in support of the non-Boer colonists there. He and all his followers had rapidly been killed or captured, but Britain had been held responsible for this hostile action. Moreover, when Alfred Milner was appointed Governor of the Cape Colony in 1897, it was his declared intention to recover for Britain both Transvaal and the Orange Free State, just as Jameson had attempted to do. Meanwhile, much of the colossal wealth of the Rand gold and diamond mines was being exploited by mainly British and German 'Uitlanders', or foreigners, who did not have a vote under Boer rule.

Most of 1899 was occupied with acrimonious negotiations between Paul Kruger for Transvaal and the British Government on behalf of the Uitlanders. Milner was deeply involved, and took a more belligerent line with the Boers, doing all that he could to provoke them into invading the Cape and neighbouring British-controlled Natal. He did not have long to wait. President Kruger had been amassing great quantities of French and German armaments of the most modern kind, and had every confidence in the skill and prowess of his Boer commandos.

The Colonial Secretary in London, Joe Chamberlain, tried to bring about a joint British–Boer inquiry into the Transvaal franchise negotiations in late July 1899, but Kruger was having none of that, and to Milner's relief was clearly hell-bent on war with Britain. The second Boer War, as it came to be known, broke out on 12 October 1899.

The autumn of 1899 was a busy time for the Prince of Wales. He had not only to act as host to his nephew, Emperor Wilhelm II of Germany, whom the Princess of Wales loathed – he was a guest at Sandringham for three days in November – but also to deal with the consequences of the early defeats suffered by the British armies in South Africa. The Boer War aroused a great deal of hostility against Britain among the European powers, especially France, and the Kaiser, who fancied himself as a great military authority, was anxious to give advice to his uncle.

All this prohibited the Prince from seeing as much of Alice Keppel as he wished. At the same time, Britain was overwhelmed by a tidal wave of patriotism and an eagerness to contribute to the war effort against the hated Kruger. Hundreds of women offered their services to the FANYS: First Aid Nursing Yeomanry Service. Offers were made to hand over private yachts to the country to act as hospital ships.

In London society there were no greater patriots than the Keyser sisters, and when at a social occasion Agnes took advantage of the Prince of Wales's presence to ask his advice on what they could do to support the nation's war effort, the Prince was prompt in his response, almost as if he had been considering the matter before Agnes had raised it.

'Why not,' he remarked in an historic question that was to have profound consequences, 'convert your house into a hospital for wounded officers when they are returned to this country?'

Agnes, it is recorded, protested that she and her sister had no nursing experience. She was told that this was not necessary. Like everything else, nursing experience could be bought – nurses could be found and paid – and, with their Keyser connections, they could no doubt persuade surgeons and consultants to offer their services, as well as their advice on the equipment and servicing of the new hospital, free of charge.

The pressure of patriotic fervour was such that, within only a few weeks, the Keyser sisters converted their home at 17 Grosvenor Crescent into a small hospital. It had twelve beds, three of them 'doubles', with a basic operating theatre and a staff of six hand-picked nurses. Agnes kept the Prince of Wales informed of progress. By December 1899 the Keyser sisters' hospital was ready, and the Prince was prepared to conduct a royal opening ceremony.

Agnes Keyser, who liked to have everything 'all shipshape and Bristol fashion', realized that, although she had already bought the appropriate uniform of starched linen, she had no title. She therefore consulted the Prince of Wales on this rather important matter:

'What am I to call myself, sir?'

Without hesitation he told her. 'You should be called Sister Agnes.'

So that was that. If the Prince of Wales was to call Agnes 'Sister' that was sufficient.

Through their numerous social connections, the sisters let it be known that 'Sister Agnes's' Hospital was open and ready to receive any officer casualties from South Africa.

In the last days of 1899, Sister Agnes wrote to General Evelyn Wood VC, Adjutant-General of the Army, to acquaint him formally with the information that the Hospital was open and ready to receive officer patients. In a letter dated the first day of the new century, Field Marshal Wood replied:

Dear Sister Agnes,

On behalf of Lords Lansdowne and Wolseley, I accept with much gratitude your very generous offer, and the Director General of the Army Medical Department has telegraphed to Cape Town to inform the Medical Officer in charge of the base hospital of the hospitality which any sick or wounded officer can, if they like, receive.

Yours sincerely,

Evelyn Wood

A week later Sister Agnes made contact with the Disembarkation Officer at Southampton, asking him to make known to any sick or wounded officers who passed through the port on arrival from South Africa of the availability of beds and nursing at her home in Belgravia. The reply was prompt:

Southampton 10th January 1900

Colonel Stacpole is in receipt of Miss Keyser's kind letter of 8th inst. which he will shew to every sick or wounded officer from South Africa and will always inform Miss Keyser by wire when necessary on the subject.

It was not long before the first hospital ships were sailing for England. The Boers proved themselves every bit as accomplished at fighting as they had at the Battle of Majuba Hill in the first Boer War, a humiliating British defeat. Kruger's men penetrated deep into Natal, besieging on the way Mafeking, Kimberley and Ladysmith, and they won notable victories at Stormberg, Modderrivier and Colenso. Many British were killed or wounded in these early conflicts; the number of wounded for the whole war was in excess of twenty-three thousand.

At Colenso, south of Ladysmith on the River Tulega, Dr Frederick Treves, the Queen's surgeon who had come straight from Harley Street, was in charge of Number 4 Field Hospital. On the day of the battle, the likely outcome of which was thought not to be in doubt, he was ordered to go at once to Naval Gun Hill. He could hear the sound of battle ahead – rifle and pom-pom fire. Far from gaining the expected easy victory over their opponents, General Redvers Buller's men – the 1st Connaught Rangers, the 2nd Dublin Fusiliers, the 1st Inniskillins, and the 1st Devons among them – were outmanoeuvred and forced to retreat across the veld, suffering terrible casualties on the way. Thomas Pakenham, in his magisterial history of the Boer War, describes, with Treves himself, the aftermath.

> The battle was over – if such an abortive affair could be called a battle at all. The struggle for the lives of the wounded was only beginning. Dr Treves . . . watched the lines of ambulance wagons rocking and groaning over the uneven veld like staggering men. Would that dismal procession never end? Treves could hardly believe that it was only a few hours before that the men had marched out to battle in the dew of the morning. Now they were 'burnt a brown red by the sun, their faces were covered with dust and sweat, and were in many cases blistered by the heat . . . the blue army shirts were stiff with blood. Some had helmets and some were bare-headed. All seemed dazed, weary and depressed.'
>
> It was here, in the small circle of field hospitals, that the horrors of the whole battlefield now seemed to be concentrated. Treves, an experienced surgeon, felt his stomach turn at some of the sights. Everywhere lay the khaki helmets, crushed, bloodstained and riddled with holes. Some of the men were delirious. They rolled off the stretchers and kicked about on the ground. One man, paralysed below the waist by a bullet in the spine, kept raising his head, staring with wonder at the limbs he could neither move nor feel. The earth seemed to be covered with groaning men. In the evening, it began to rain . . .[3]

Those officers who survived the long train journey down to Durban, followed by treatment in the base hospital there and then the lengthy voyage home in the hospital ship, were among the first to be greeted by Sister Agnes at 17 Grosvenor Crescent.

These first wounded officers arrived in early February 1900. Sister Agnes herself met them at the door and helped them from the horse ambulances which had brought them from Waterloo station. The absence of a lift posed some difficulties but there were strong arms to draw on among the male staff.

Each officer was accompanied by a case sheet, giving his medical history from the time he was wounded. At this stage of the war, which was too mobile for much artillery to be used, nearly all of them were suffering from gunshot wounds. Most of the officers had already been operated on when necessary, at field dressing stations or in hospital at Durban, but if an elaborate operating theatre was required, one was available at nearby St George's Hospital.*

Week by week, the sisters improved the routine of running their Hospital. Fanny was a diligent administrator and was not often seen in the wards, while Agnes supervised the nursing and comforted her charges – 'my boys' as she referred to them, though some were brigadiers from famous regiments. At the same time, if there had to be an operation under gas, she made it a point of honour to be present both when the patient went under and when he came round, holding his hand in her own tiny hands. Many an officer testified to the comfort this gave him.

Sister Agnes also supervised the finances of the Hospital and took on herself the dual responsibilities of keeping pace with the expenses and maintaining the pressure on the benefactors, a duty she followed with uninhibited enthusiasm all her life. It became clear from the beginning that while there was no limit to Agnes's determination and zeal in following up any source of finance, whether individual or corporate, she was equally loath to demonstrate what she felt to be 'cheap self-advertisement'. It was a formula that reflected her personal characteristics. The fact that it worked uncommonly well for over forty years is sufficient confirmation of its efficacy.

This lack of self-advertisement had one consequence not entirely favourable to the Hospital. Outside the London medical profession and the hierarchy of the War Office, very few people knew that it existed. Sister Agnes was not concerned with contributions from ordinary people (or 'the common people' as she would call them). Bankers, stockbrokers like her own father, captains of industry and the like, from whom she would expect at least a donation of £100 or, better still, a covenant for the sum for five years, were her targets. But the main costs of running 17 Grosvenor Crescent at this time were still met by Agnes and Fanny themselves.

The Prince of Wales visited the Hospital frequently, sometimes

---

* Now the Lanesborough Hotel.

coming in the evening when he would dine alone with Agnes. They exchanged gossip of a harmless nature, and the Prince could safely confide in his hostess. She could not prohibit His Royal Highness from smoking his huge cigars, but she did warn him of the harm he was doing to his lungs, as was only too clear from the appalling coughing to which he was subject.

Bertie, as Sister Agnes was encouraged to call him, enjoyed the relaxed nature of these evenings. He even enjoyed the simple dishes that were put before him, Agnes correctly assuming that he ate far too much excessively rich food, whether at home in Marlborough House or when dining out. Irish stew, followed by rice pudding and a baked apple, was often on her menu – and the Prince consumed these with the same relish as if they were grouse stuffed with truffles and garnished with a rich liqueur sauce.

The Prince of Wales normally went to stay in Biarritz when the season was over, but in 1900 the British were so unpopular in France because of the Boer War and the Fashoda incident which had earlier humiliated France, that members of the Royal Family were advised to keep clear of the country. So instead of Biarritz with Alice Keppel for the Prince, it was Denmark, which he found very dull, with the Princess who was by contrast delighted to see her land of birth.

Disaster followed disaster in South Africa. The world mocked the most powerful nation for its humiliation by a few thousand Boer farmers, although in fact there were far more Boers, far better armed, than the British had estimated. Moreover, they were brilliantly led and fighting on familiar terrain. Colenso marked the end for the British of 'Black Week'. There were, however, many more setbacks ahead, and it was clearly seen that this was not to be just another of those minor colonial wars that had periodically broken out during much of Queen Victoria's reign. Reinforcements were hurried out to the Cape, including Australian and Canadian volunteers.

The Queen was in Scotland when the news of 'Black Week' arrived at Balmoral. Her journal for this time reflects her depression and dismay. When she learned from her youngest daughter, Princess Beatrice, of the three humiliating defeats in South Africa, she was heard to say, 'Now perhaps they will take my advice, and send out Lord Roberts and Lord Kitchener.' And so they did.

Roberts landed at the Cape from the fastest available ship, together with Kitchener who had been appointed his Chief of Staff. Before long the tide began to turn. The siege of Ladysmith was lifted, causing great relief and excitement at home. In the same month of February 1900 the British scored their first outright victory at Paardeberg, and in the following month Roberts captured the Boer city of Bloemfontein. Mafeking was relieved in May, and for twenty-four hours Britain went mad with excitement, leading to the adoption of the term 'Mafficking', meaning an 'extravagant and boisterous cele-bration'. Buller redeemed himself by taking Pretoria, after relieving Ladysmith.

All these successes were welcome news for the British Government. But the casualties were heavy, and several times a week hospital ships docked at Southampton. No matter how small was her Hospital, Sister Agnes was working very long hours for a woman in her late forties. As soon as her patients were fit to travel, they were put on a train bound for convalescence homes, while back at Grosvenor Crescent the beds were occupied again as soon as they were remade.

The Princess of Wales visited the wounded in London hospitals in August, including the officers at 17 Grosvenor Crescent. Sister Agnes took Her Royal Highness, accompanied by her daughter Victoria, to every bedside, and noted how sympathetically this Princess talked to the wounded.

Before leaving for Balmoral and grouse shooting, Princess Alexandra dispatched a telegram to Sister Agnes:

15 August 1900

Victoria and I thank the hospital and its kind inmates for the beautiful flowers and good wishes for our journey and hope for a speedy recovery of the poor invalids.

Alexandra

During the remainder of the year, Johannesburg fell to the British, and Kruger fled to Europe. Still there was no sign of a complete sur-render from the Boers, who formed themselves into small but lethal guerrilla brigades, ranging over the veld and attacking British outposts.

Not until the end of May 1902 was a peace agreement signed. The killing had stopped at last. Meanwhile much had been happening at home and, in its own small way, to Sister Agnes's Hospital.

CHAPTER 2

The King Offers His Name

Q UEEN VICTORIA WAS eighty-one in May 1900. 'God has been very merciful and supported me, but my trials and anxieties have been manifold and I feel tired and upset by all I have gone through this winter and spring,' she dictated, her eyes being too weak to write.

Scotland usually cheered her, but not this year. Even the telegrams announcing victories in South Africa failed to lift her spirits. She felt tired all the time, but none of her doctors could diagnose any specific ailment. Then her second son, Alfred – 'Affie', very dear to her – died suddenly of throat cancer. His death was followed by that of her soldier grandson, Christian Victor, of disease in Pretoria. Finally, and most grievous of all, her lady-in-waiting and friend of almost half a century, Lady Churchill, died of a heart attack.

The Queen was at Osborne on the Isle of Wight in January 1901 when it became clear that she was not going to recover. Messages of goodwill arrived from around the world. Even Kruger sent a telegram from South Africa, to which he had returned, calling for her prompt recovery. The Queen's children and grandchildren assembled at Osborne. The Prince of Wales had been much concerned by the deaths in the family, and had gone to Germany for his brother Affie's funeral. He was also deeply depressed by the condition of his eldest sister, Vicky, the Dowager Empress Frederick, who was also dying of cancer, a fact kept from the Queen.

On his return he was cheered by a house party at Chatsworth where Alice Keppel was a fellow guest. He was back in London when he received a telegram, on 18 January, advising him to come to Osborne owing to his mother's serious condition. That evening he invited himself to dinner with Sister Agnes. The usual plain fare was put before him, and they talked of the imminent death of the Queen. At one point Bertie declared that he felt quite unworthy to succeed her. Sister Agnes reassured him, pouring at the same time a rare (for her) glass of brandy for them both.

Queen Victoria died at 6.30 p.m. on 22 January 1901 with many members of her large family about her bed. The next morning King Edward VII travelled to London to attend the Accession Council. The oath was administered by the Archbishop of Canterbury, after which there was a speech by the new sovereign.

The King had been in the wings for more than half a century through periods of personal popularity and unpopularity, and there were those (including the editor of *The Times*) who had misgivings about his capacity for the job. But if Sister Agnes could have been among the Privy Councillors present on this occasion, her belief in the King would have been confirmed by the speech he delivered on his accession:

> The King set the tone of his entire reign by delivering, to an audience of about 150 people, a perfect and impromptu eight minutes' speech, based entirely upon intuition. Because it had been assumed that the King would speak on such an occasion from a prepared text, or at least from notes, no record was taken; and the published version of that speech, which had to be reconstructed from memory, was considered less remarkable than the original. Even so it was most impressive; and the King made a moving and brilliant reference to his father. He did not, he said, undervalue the name of Albert which he bore, but there could be only one Albert 'who by universal consent is, I think deservedly, known by the name of Albert the Good . . .'[1]

Although the Boer War was at last over there remained many sick and wounded officers requiring attention. By 1901, the word had spread among the regiments of the special comforts and attention enjoyed by those who were admitted to Sister Agnes's Hospital. It was certainly the only military hospital where a formally dressed butler came round to take orders for drinks in the evening – all at no charge to the patient. Moreover, the nurses had clearly been hand picked, and while regulations were strictly adhered to, the presence of the cheerful, active little figure of Sister Agnes herself was always a pleasure and a comfort.

His accession to the throne in no way diminished the King's personal interest in the Hospital, and he made frequent visits, by himself and with Queen Alexandra – and from time to time, on an informal basis, with Alice Keppel. The visits were sometimes reported in the Press. As a reward for all their work during the Boer War, ninety-one of the Hospital's past patients clubbed together and presented the Keyser sisters with two large silver salvers, which can still be seen in the entrance to the Hospital today. Above the ninety-one signatures are inscribed the following words:

PRESENTED TO MISS A. KEYSER [OR MISS F. KEYSER] BY THE UNDERMENTIONED OFFICERS WHO HAVE BEEN PATIENTS IN KING EDWARD'S HOSPITAL AT VARIOUS TIMES SINCE THE COMMENCEMENT OF THE WAR IN SOUTH AFRICA AS A MARK OF THEIR GRATITUDE FOR THE VERY GREAT KINDNESS AND CARE INVARIABLY SHOWN TO THEM THERE. DECEMBER 31st 1901.

A few months earlier, the following announcement had appeared in the *London Gazette*:

War Office, August 9, 1901
The King has been graciously pleased
to confer the decoration of the
Royal Red Cross upon –
Miss Margaret Fanny Keyser,
Miss Agnes Keyser,
in recognition of services rendered to
the sick and wounded returned from South Africa[2]

Both sisters wore them prominently.

*

There is no documentary evidence to prove it, but it seems likely that the second phase of Sister Agnes's Hospital, after the Boer War, began during Doncaster race week in September 1903. The King always stayed at Rufford Abbey nearby as a guest of Lord and Lady Savile. At the weekend they held a big house party, which that year included both Sister Agnes and Alice Keppel. Agnes had been abroad that summer, returning at the beginning of September. She had enjoyed the four years since she and her sister had established their little twelve-bed Hospital. She had felt fulfilled and believed that she had found her vocation. Now she wondered if there could be a continuing demand in peacetime for a free hospital for indigent officers of both services.

There is a surviving letter from the old Duke of Cambridge, Queen Victoria's first cousin, Commander-in-Chief of the Army seemingly since the beginning of time, and also a close friend of Agnes. He regrets in this letter his inability to join her at Rufford Abbey: 'I am getting too old,' he writes, which was true enough. But he adds, 'How nice of you to think of establishing a little hospital of your own for Army and Navy officers,' concluding, 'Wishing you good sport and a pleasant party, I remain, Yours most sincerely and affectionately, George.'

It is on record that Sister Agnes asked the advice of the King about keeping her Hospital open, and that he said, decisively as usual, that certainly she should. It was performing a very valuable service, and she could put his name to it, thus christening for all time King Edward VII's Hospital for Officers: Sister Agnes Founder.

With the King's blessing, Agnes went into action once more with her well-known pace and enthusiasm. This time, without the pressure of a war behind her, she could afford to take the time to structure things properly. She must have a Patron, a President, a Chairman of the Council, and contributions. The Patron must, of course, be the King, and on 18 November Sister Agnes wrote to the new Prince of Wales, the King's eldest son George, at Marlborough House, inviting him to become President. His private secretary replied, 'I am desired to say that the Prince of Wales will have much pleasure in becoming President of King Edward's Hospital for Officers, and also in guaranteeing a sum of £100 if the Hospital be in need . . .'

Arthur, Duke of Connaught, the King's younger brother and an old friend of Agnes, wrote in reply to her letter, 'It will give me great pleasure to become Vice-President of your little hospital for naval and military officers. It seems to me an excellent idea, and I wish every success to the undertaking . . .'

A similar letter from the Duke of Cambridge's private secretary from Gloucester House in Park Lane confirmed that 'His Royal Highness has the greatest pleasure in accepting the position . . .'

With three members of the Royal Family in the presidential chairs and His Majesty the King as Patron, Sister Agnes could now set about – with some confidence – finding subscribers. She sensibly endeavoured to persuade them, as before, to guarantee their subscriptions for five years, and at £100 a year. In a very short time she had found twenty-four of the richest men in the land to lend their names. The King and the Prince of Wales of course headed the list, which included brewers, bankers, printers and publishers like Sir Sydney Waterlow and Lord Burnham of the *Daily Telegraph*. There were Sassoons and Rothschilds; Agnes's father; Sir Ernest Cassel, who had transformed the financial fortunes of the King; and many others. Lord Derby and Lord Burton could scarcely have noticed the loss of £500 over five years. Other prominent names from the City were Lord Farquhar and Mr Bischoffsheim, and in early 1904 there were other benefactors, including a Mrs Ada H. Lewis of Grosvenor Square who promised an annual subscription of £200.

Just as it was war in South Africa which had led to the birth of the Hospital, however, so it was the wealth of that same country which rescued it. The Hospital had saved the lives of those who had fought for the freedom of the Transvaal and Orange Free State, and in recognition of this, in 1904–5 the Randlords Julius Wernher and Alfred Beit contributed generously towards the cost of establishing the Hospital on a permanent basis. They donated £8,000, partly in cash and partly in debenture shares in Lisbon and Mexican tramways. Another partner in the business, Sir Lionel Phillips, gave £500 and yet another, a German-born South African, 'Friedie' Eckstein, donated a further thousand pounds.

This munificence resulted in King Edward conferring baronetcies on Alfred Beit and Julius Wernher, whose interest in the Hospital and

Sister Agnes remained close until Wernher's death in May 1912. (His partner, Alfred Beit, died in 1906.)

This sudden wealth decided Sister Agnes, in consultation with the King, to find new premises for the enterprise. Agnes and her sister Fanny had found it inconvenient and cramped sharing their house with the patients and staff at 17 Grosvenor Crescent. A lease was available for a house nearby at 9 Grosvenor Gardens, once the property of Lord Randolph Churchill. An immediate offer was made, and work started on its conversion into a twelve-bed hospital with operating theatre.

On 23 April 1904, the King officially opened this newly named, newly situated hospital, in an event that was marked by a brass plaque – like the salvers, to be seen in the entrance hall of the Hospital today. It reads simply:

PATRON
HIS MAJESTY THE KING

———

PRESIDENT
H.R.H. THE PRINCE OF WALES

———

VICE-PRESIDENTS
H.R.H. THE DUKE OF CONNAUGHT
H.R.H. THE DUKE OF CAMBRIDGE

THIS HOSPITAL FOR OFFICERS IN THE NAVY AND ARMY WAS FOUNDED IN JULY 1903 BY AGNES KEYSER (SISTER AGNES) WITH THE HELP OF A FEW GENEROUS FRIENDS AND WAS OPENED BY THE KING APRIL 23 1904. IT IS A CONTINUATION OF THE HOSPITAL FOR OFFICERS ORIGINATED AND MAINTAINED BY MISS KEYSER AND SISTER AGNES AT 17 GROSVENOR CRESCENT DURING THE WARS IN AFRICA AND CHINA FROM 1899 TO 1902.

Even before this official opening, Sister Agnes, uncharacteristically but perhaps at the behest of the King, seems to have invited the Press to the new Hospital for a preview. From old newspaper cuttings, we gain detailed accounts of King Edward VII's Hospital. The *Daily Telegraph*, for example, reported:

Accommodation for 12 beds is afforded in five wards containing two beds each and in two smaller wards containing one bed each.

The ground floor of the house provides an office for Sister Agnes herself, a large waiting room (the original dining room) for the friends of patients, and a nurses' dining room at the back. On the first floor the front and back drawing rooms have been thrown together, the former furnished as a luxurious sitting room for patients, the latter containing a full-sized billiard table; and a smaller room at the back is made into a sitting room for nurses. On the upper floors are the wards, and above them are bedrooms for nurses and servants. A fire escape has been fitted up, and there is an easy access to a considerable extent of the roof, on which it is the intention of Sister Agnes to try experiments in floriculture and which, whether these succeed or fail, will at least afford to those who can reach it, a view which includes a considerable extent of the gardens of Buckingham Palace.

The patients' sitting room . . . is not only very handsomely decorated and furnished, and well supplied with books, telephones and other comforts, but will contain many decorative articles which have been presented by various supporters.

Mention should also be made that all the plate required for the hospital has been presented by Messrs Carrington, of Regent Street.

The ward furniture, which has been specially made by Messrs Druce, of course, is of similar type and is so constructed as to offer no coigns of vantage for the lodgement of dust. It is covered with white enamel and, together with the whiteness of the walls, affords that promise of absolute and perfect cleanliness which modern physicians and surgeons have learnt to regard as one of the essentials of successful treatment.

The operating theatre has been fitted up with every possible contrivance for facilitating the work of the surgeons; and its completion alone has cost nearly, or quite, a thousand pounds.

The medical and surgical staff of the Hospital will be nominated by the King, but the nominations have not yet been made public . . .

The list of honorary medical staff was eventually published from Buckingham Palace on 6 July 1904. It was headed by two distinguished consulting surgeons, Sir Thomas Smith Bt., Hon. Serjeant Surgeon to the King; and Sir Frederick Treves, back from South Africa, who had recently saved the King's life by operating on an infected appendix, a radical operation at the time. Among the twenty-four distinguished doctors and surgeons on the list were several from the team who provided their services during the Boer War.

Most accounts in the Press emphasized the link between King Edward VII's Hospital and Osborne House on the Isle of Wight, which the King, who disliked the place, had converted into a convalescent home soon after he inherited it from his mother. One report described King Edward VII's Hospital as 'a metropolitan adjunct to the convalescent home at Osborne'. Osborne and King Edward VII's Hospital did have two things in common: they were established at roughly the same time, and (as the King saw it) they were both his inspiration. But Sister Agnes saw things differently, and did not like her establishment to be associated with any other. She had to keep her opinions to herself and tread carefully, but over the next few years she gradually and discreetly sent fewer convalescents to Osborne House. There is on record a rather wounded letter from the Matron at Osborne to Sister Agnes, mildly complaining about this. Sister Agnes replied firmly and at once, denying the accusation. In reality, she had nothing against Osborne House except the assumption that her 'boys' would automatically go there to convalesce.

The opening of the Hospital coincided with the signing of the Entente Cordiale, and France was very much in the King's mind that spring. This important historical settlement was another event about which Edward VII felt very proprietorial. A report in the contemporary *Daily Express* tells of an additional, if small, contribution to the Entente:

When the King was visiting his own little private hospital for officers in Grosvenor Gardens, he said, 'We must have the French doctors down here,' and straight away he issued an invitation by telegram.

So yesterday afternoon a body of French doctors [thirty in all] went down to Grosvenor Gardens and were received by Sister Agnes.

The visitors were conducted over the most diminutive but most perfect hospital in the world. There was no nook or cranny into which the Frenchmen did not penetrate or enquire about. And all of them were enchanted.

Some of the Frenchmen thought that because the sister and nurses wore uniform, they belonged to some religious order, and were vowed to celibacy. When they learned that they were not they were astonished and at tea in the committee room they made ample amends by many compliments.

It was all in considerable contrast with the time – only a year or two earlier – when the Royal Family were advised not to visit France because of that country's hostility. This reversal of attitude was mainly thanks to King Edward VII himself.

It was not long after the King formally opened the Hospital at its new site that he offered Sister Agnes a key to the little back gate into the Buckingham Palace gardens, suggesting that she should use them at any time. The King himself could be seen there frequently, regularly after breakfast before starting work in his study. Sometimes he was by himself, sometimes with an equerry or his private secretary, Lord Stamfordham, and sometimes with the Queen. Being a man of regular habits, he always walked once round the lake in the same clockwise direction, briskly and without pause.

Sister Agnes often joined him when he was by himself, bustling along beside him as her little dog, Needle, darted here and there with the King's fox terrier, Caesar. The King and Agnes exchanged the gossip of the day, both having their own sources, and both relying on the discretion of the other.

Sister Agnes was often at Sandringham as a guest of the King. She knew many of her fellow guests from her social life before the Boer War and was a great authority on *Burke's Peerage*. She 'loved a lord' and was in turn liked and admired not only because of her evident close friendship with the King, but also because of her Hospital, her liveliness, her eccentricity and her wealth – not necessarily in that order.

When it was time for the Court to move north to Balmoral for the grouse season in August, she was often a guest there, too. The Prince and Princess of Wales were especially fond of her, and loved seeing her striding out over the heather, a diminutive figure afraid of nothing, and 'wearing bright mauve and an orange wig'. Wigs were widely worn at this time, of course, but those of orange colour were not often seen.

CHAPTER 3

Death of a King, and an Archduke

I N THE HOSPITAL'S fifteenth year, Sister Agnes could note with satisfaction the neat figure of 1,500 patients treated since she and her sister had opened the doors of their house to some of the first officers wounded in South Africa. One hundred a year. The Hospital had not always been full but there had never been a shortage of sick (rather than wounded) officers since the end of that war.

In the world outside 9 Grosvenor Gardens there had been plenty of international crises and conflicts, none for the present immediately threatening Britain and her Empire. But Edward VII ruled over a restless and sometimes dangerous period at home. Politics were turned on their head by the general election of 1906, when the Liberal Party enjoyed a landslide victory. Some of their radical reforms were opposed by the unelected House of Lords and thrown out. Prime Minister Henry Campbell-Bannerman dissolved Parliament and threatened to flood the Lords with peers of his nomination.

Another domestic upheaval concerned the suffragettes and their campaign for votes for women which had violent repercussions, but which failed throughout Edward VII's reign, and for many years after. Sister Agnes, conservative and traditionalist, thought the whole thing tiresome and disgraceful.

Although Britain was not at war, the threat of war breaking out hovered over the country like a dark and menacing cloud. The chief cause for concern was the German Emperor, Queen Victoria's eldest grandson, Kaiser Wilhelm II, and the nationalism he inflamed. He became increasingly unbalanced and dangerous, envious of his uncle, Edward VII, and of the British Empire and Royal Navy. He used his acquisition of 'a place in the sun', as he called his colonial empire, as a justification for building a navy so large that it threatened Britain's control of the seas, which she had held since the Battle of Trafalgar more than a hundred years earlier. The Dreadnought race, as the competition between the two navies was dubbed, after the Royal Navy's revolutionary battleship of 1906, cost the two nations millions of pounds.

Even before King Edward VII's Hospital was reopened in its new locality, Britain came uncomfortably close to war with Russia again when the Russian fleet opened fire on British fishing vessels in the North Sea and sank one; they had mistaken them for Japanese torpedo boats. The fleet was on its way to the Far East to try to regain control of the sea there in Russia's war with Japan. A British fleet shadowed the Russians down the Channel and across the Bay of Biscay while Britain demanded an apology and reparations, at first refused by the Russians. It appeared that the Russian Admiral had failed to report the incident to his seniors. King Edward did not lower the heat of the crisis by commenting to his Foreign Secretary, 'If the Russian Admiral continues on his way without even communicating with his own Government, we really have a right to stop him.' However, at length terms of compensation were agreed, and the Russian fleet continued on its way slowly to Japan, and to virtual annihilation in battle.

Soon after peace terms had been agreed between the Russian Empire and Japan (with whom Britain had a Treaty of Friendship), other crises threatened the peace in Europe. War actually did break out in 1908 when ever-aggressive Austria–Hungary struck at Bosnia and Herzegovina and annexed these two nations. Almost every day the newspapers reported the invention of terrible new weapons of war. Battleships and their guns increased in size, while military and naval manoeuvres were carried out constantly and ostentatiously by the great powers.

King Edward was deeply concerned about this international state of affairs, and did his best as a peacemaker, especially with France and Russia. Only with Germany and Austria–Hungary could he make no progress. At the suppers which he continued to enjoy with Sister Agnes, he sometimes poured out his heart to her, although he was always conscious of the need not to bore her.

For her part Sister Agnes revealed an intelligent interest in foreign affairs and followed the King's sometimes rather tortuous efforts in the cause of peace. For instance, in 1903 he calculated that it would be most appropriate to begin his historic visits to the King of Italy and the President of France by arriving on the Continent by sea at the Portuguese capital of Lisbon. One of the reasons for this was his friendship with and trust in the discretion of both King Carlos II of Portugal and the Marquis de Soveral, the Portuguese Minister in London. Sister Agnes was one of the few people (and they did not at first include the Queen or the Foreign Minister), who was privy to King Edward's plans. The visit to Lisbon secured even tighter bonds between the two Kings.

Then, in February 1908, King Edward's old Portuguese friend was shot by left-wing assassins, together with the Crown Prince. King Edward was not afraid of assassins – he never had been – but he

> became increasingly disturbed by the violence and unrest. Perhaps Balfour [Arthur Balfour, British statesman] was right in supposing that England had caught the Continental disease, which had produced massacres in St Petersburg, riots in Vienna, and Socialist processions in Berlin . . . the King himself believed that his grandson would never reign and that the red flag would flutter above the Mall.[1]

Before its re-establishment in Grosvenor Gardens, and its formal opening by the King, little had appeared in the Press about King Edward VII's Hospital. But during 1904, particular numbers of weekly magazines and daily newspapers carried articles stressing the good work already done by Sister Agnes in the past, and the royal connections and high social standing of the Keyser sisters.

By 1906 it became necessary to increase the number of staff. The Prince of Wales, as Patron, wrote approvingly of the success of the Hospital which had brought about this need.

Sir Arthur Bigge, his Private Secretary, added, 'His Royal Highness hopes to have an opportunity of again visiting your Hospital. He thinks it is wonderful that such a large number of officers have already been nursed, and so many operations performed since you so nobly started your work.' The Duke of Connaught, writing from Windsor Castle, echoed these sentiments.

It was at this time – 1906 – that the only portrait of Sister Agnes was painted. It was in the form of a three-quarter-length study, emphasizing her narrow waist and drawing out the beauty of her firm but kindly face. The artist was Miss Maud Coleridge and a reproduction hangs in the entrance hall in Beaumont Street today: the original met a violent end in 1941. Considerable pressure had to be brought to bear on the subject for her to pose for the artist, but she looks cheerful enough. The portrait was reproduced in most of the illustrated and society magazines of the time. The caption in one of them read, 'Miss Agnes Keyser, better known, perhaps, as Sister Agnes, has earned fame as a great public benefactor, and gave the whole of her time, her work and money to the foundation of King Edward VII's Hospital for Officers. She was one of the New Year guests of the King and Queen at Sandringham.'

Almost half a century after he had been a patient at Grosvenor Gardens in 1906, under observation for a possible broken neck, a naval officer recalled:

> While I was there Sister Agnes suggested to a young midshipman that she would like to know how much money 'one day's' pay from every officer in HM services would bring in. With the total, she said she could double the size of the Hospital. I don't know when the move was made to Grosvenor Crescent [1919]. I paid them a visit at this address, and had the pleasure of again meeting Sister Agnes, and her sister (who managed the library and other jobs outside the medical work). I remember there were two small requests made to all officers on leaving. One was to give a photograph to the hospital albums, and the other to give a book to the library . . .
>
> Yours sincerely,
> Captain G. M. Skinner RN

One officer at this time not only gave a book to the library; he also wrote a long poem in tribute to the Hospital, which he had printed and bound. The opening quatrains (there are more than twenty) are quoted here, along with the closing three.

ELEGY

If you're strolling round idle in London
Midst the home of the rich and the great
You may happen one day in a casual way
On the place of which feebly I prate.

'Sister Agnes's' that's what it's known as
By those, the select chosen few
Who've been there – 9 Grosvenor Gardens,
To cabmen and strangers too.

It's home for the sick and the wounded
Of the Army and Navy as well.
In peace or in war you'll find by the door
A clamouring crowd round the bell,

Seeking entrance. In chairs and on crutches
In thousands and millions they come;
They know a good thing when they see one,
Though they're lame, halt, blind and dumb . . .

Oh thou soldier, whoever you may be,
Be you Guardsman, proud Lancer, Dragoon
Horse, Foot, or Gun, from wherever the sun
Sinks down, from where rises the moon.

Be ye sick, be ye footsore or weary,
Be ye wounded in battle's hard Strife,
Come rest at this haven from suffering,
Sister Agnes will bring you to life.

Sister Agnes, the thanks of the Army,
Of the Navy, the Nation, are due
To one who thus cares for their sufferers,
Long Life and all fortune to you.

A. G. SOAMES, Coldstream Guards. October 3rd, 1908.

In March 1908, while Queen Alexandra's sister Minnie (the Dowager Empress Marie Feodorovna of Russia) was staying with her in London, they made a visit to King Edward VII's Hospital, hospitals being a special interest of the Dowager Empress. That 'they were much pleased with all they saw' was confirmed by a letter from the Queen at Buckingham Palace:

Dear 'Sister Agnes',

I am so glad to find from your letter that my sister's and my visit to the Hospital gave you two sisters as well as the invalid officers pleasure.

I must now tell you how delighted we were with all we saw, and the excellent management under your able direction.

I must say that all the new improvements, lift and all, were first rate. Hoping that all the officers are doing well.

Yours sincerely,

Alexandra

This is the first reference to the installation of a lift, which had become necessary. So, no more lugging stretchers around the many bends in the stairs!

By 1908 the five-year covenants signed in 1903–4 were becoming exhausted and Sister Agnes began the considerable task of appealing for a renewal to cover the following five years. Only three people failed her, Lords Derby, Neuman and Sandwich, all of whom complained of the calls made on their funds. The Duke of Connaught, for reasons best known to himself, offered only five shillings a year. But the old steady supporters all signed up, including the King and the Prince of Wales, Sir Ernest Cassel, the Rothschilds, brother Charles Keyser, the Sassoons, Sir Everard Hambro, and Lords Iveagh and Strathcona who straight away added for good measure donations of £250 and £500 respectively.

All this was eminently satisfactory, but Sister Agnes conceived the idea of an overall but voluntary annual subscription from every Army and Navy officer of five shillings a year. This was not a success, and she quietly let the fact be known to certain acquaintances in the newspaper industry (and she knew pretty well all of them).

This produced some sharp comments. 'A Gunner Major', no doubt a 'plant', wrote the following letter to one newspaper:

> Sir – it is simply disgraceful that officers should have been so backward in coming forward with a paltry 5s a year in answer to Sister Agnes's appeal. I cannot believe it is through a desire not to subscribe, but through mere slackness. I have asked one or two 'subs' why they have not done so; their answers were, 'Oh, I never heard of it', or 'I forgot', or like one who thought it was a begging letter . . . I am thankful to say I have never had to avail myself of Sister Agnes's hospitality, but I know many men who have done so, and not one but has reason to thank her from the bottom of his heart for all she has done . . .

A severe editorial in another newspaper began:

> Some months ago we called attention to the special appeal being made to officers of the Army on behalf of the King Edward's Hospital for Officers. It is disappointing to learn that the appeal then made has not realised expectations, and that unless further support is given it may be necessary to close the hospital . . .

This and other publicity for the appeal and the Hospital awoke consciences in the members of the two services, but not to the extent Sister Agnes had anticipated, and she remained largely dependent on the five-year covenants of the Hospital's affluent friends, and the advice of wise and worldly men of the City like Sir Julius Wernher and Sir Ernest Cassel for making the best use of the Hospital's capital resources.

Finally, and to make doubly sure that the Hospital would never be at risk of closure, Sister Agnes handed over to its Trustees these securities from her private property:

£10,072 Trustees and Securities Insurance Corporation 4½% Cum. Pref. Stock.

£3,960 New Zealand Loan and Mercantile Agency 4½% Debenture Stock.

£900 Australian Estates and Mercantile Agency 4% Debenture Stock.

£2,385 John Barker & Co. Ltd 5½% Cum. Pref. Shares of £5 each.

£1,000 Buenos Aires and Pacific Railway Co.

The Deed of Declaration of Trust in respect of these securities was dated 5 June 1909. By the terms of this deed, Sister Agnes retained extensive powers for herself over the finances of the Hospital, independent of the other Trustees.

The attempt to achieve a broader if nominal subscription from officers of the two services had one curious and disturbing consequence. Sister Agnes heard rumours that someone was discouraging naval officers from using the facilities of the Hospital. She therefore dispatched a letter to the Fourth Sea Lord, Admiral Sir Alfred Leigh Winsloe KCB, on 16 December 1909:

Dear Sir Alfred,

I want to tell you at once about a matter that is troubling me in connection with this hospital. You and Sir Wilmot Fawkes [Commander-in-Chief, Plymouth, and one-time ADC to Queen Victoria] are kindly trying to help us by getting subscriptions from Naval Officers collected in the easiest way for them and the best way for us, with the understanding that a Naval Officer could come here if he wished. I find, however, that this is not always the case.

My point is this – I could not possibly take subscriptions from Naval Officers unless I am sure that the authorities would make no difficulties when an officer applied for sick leave to come here.

Why should officers be asked to help to keep up this hospital unless it could be of real use to them when they need it?

Believe me,

Yours sincerely,

Sister Agnes

Fawkes and Winsloe had an urgent talk about this matter. Fawkes then sent a long letter to his senior admiral, a copy of which was sent to Sister Agnes:

Dear Sister Agnes,

The enclosed from Sir William Fawkes *I* think settles all your qualms and I agree with everything he has written about the young officers.

Compliments of the season followed. Fawkes's explanation was that possibly 'some of the surgeons in the Navy think that an operation can as well be performed in a Naval, as in a London hospital . . .' That is to say, professional jealousy was perhaps behind it all.

That may well have been the case but it is worth remembering that the Board of Admiralty was in an unhappy condition at this time under the First Sea Lord, Admiral Lord Fisher of Kilverstone – 'Jackie' Fisher. Fisher was a great divider and had bitter enemies at every level of the service: you were either in or out of 'the Fishpond'. Winsloe was very much a pro-Fisher man, and the trouble may have been stirred up to discredit him in the eyes of the King, who was also a pro-Fisher man. Fisher was forced to retire in 1910, *after* the death of Edward VII, and he never forgave his enemies, like Admiral Lord Charles Beresford or Admiral Sir Reginald Custance.

The real cause of this unfortunate business will probably never be known, but it certainly showed Sister Agnes as a fearless defender of her Hospital.

In any case the disturbance was soon to be driven from her mind by the dreadful blow caused by the death of the monarch whose name her Hospital carried.

Nothing favours the reputation of King Edward VII so much as his monarchical achievements of the last years of his reign. Along with Alice Keppel, no one appreciated this more than Sister Agnes, not even the admirable but somewhat distant Queen Alexandra. And, finally, no one but his father, Prince Albert, had continued to attend to his business duties so close to his death.

In March 1910, earlier than usual and without Alice Keppel, the King set out for Biarritz. *En route*, he stayed overnight in Paris, where he had remained popular with the people since 1903. Ever a theatre lover, he went one evening to a new play, Edmond Rostand's *Chanticler*. He found it 'stupid and childish' and the temperature of the theatre 'oppressive'. Coming out into the cold air after the performance he caught a chill 'with a threatening of bronchitis'. His accompanying doctor even became fearful for his life. But with Edward's usual rugged stoicism, he recovered well enough to continue his journey to Biarritz.

The sea air of 'Doctor' Biarritz completed his cure, although the King still coughed terribly and bronchitis constantly threatened. A fresh sense of urgency began to govern his actions as if he sensed he had not long to live. For the first time, he did not stop at Paris on the way home from Biarritz, telling 'Fritz' Ponsonby, his secretary, that he must try to clear up the political mess at home concerning the crisis over the House of Lords.

He arrived at Victoria station at 6 p.m. on 27 April and, facing the dread prospect of an evening without occupation, ordered his box to be made ready at the opera house. *Rigoletto* was a great deal better than *Chanticler*. But he was observed by his old friend Lord Redesdale, viewing him from the stalls, to be 'very tired and worn'.

For the next two days the King caught up with his work, and gave audiences to a number of people, including the Prime Minister, Herbert Asquith, and Field Marshal Kitchener. They all noted his briskness of manner combined with evidence of weariness and illness. One visitor begged him to take to his bed. The King replied, 'No, I shall not give in – I shall work to the end. Of what use is it to be alive if one cannot work.'

On Saturday 30 April the King took the train to Sandringham for the weekend. He was particularly anxious to see for himself how far some radical changes in the gardens had advanced since his departure for Biarritz. On Sunday after divine service he spent some time in the gardens. It was bitterly cold and wet. When he returned to Buckingham Palace on the Monday he was feeling very poorly.

Whether he wanted to say goodbye to Sister Agnes or simply enjoy the reassurance of her company, will never be known, but he invited himself to supper with her at Grosvenor Gardens. At least she would not fuss over him, however much he coughed, and would not press unwanted food on him. Half-way through the evening, however, she left him briefly to telephone Buckingham Palace and report his dreadful condition, suggesting that his carriage should be sent and the doctors alerted.

The onset of bronchitis gave the King little rest that night, and his doctor, Sir Francis Laking, tried unsuccessfully to keep him in bed. The King had business to attend to. 'Teddy' Roosevelt, the ex-President of the United States, would shortly be arriving, and the King wished to discuss arrangements with the American Ambassador, Whitelaw Reid. His Excellency was appalled by the King's condition, and later wrote, 'Our talk was interrupted by spasms of coughing, and I found that he was suffering from a good many symptoms of bronchial asthma . . . It seems to me that these attacks are coming on more frequently within the last two years and that they are becoming harder to shake off.'[2]

King Edward was prevailed upon not to go out. No opera, no visits to Grosvenor Gardens. Sighing, one imagines, with the prospect of boredom, he invited Alice Keppel and the amusing socialite Mrs Willy James to dinner and bridge with his secretary Ponsonby making up the four.

Queen Alexandra arrived home, summoned from a holiday in Corfu, and the other members of the family, including the Prince of Wales, gathered at the palace, just as they had done nine years earlier at Osborne House for the King's mother. True to his promise, he did work to the end, or until it was impossible to do so any longer. The Queen, generous in spirit as always, invited Alice Keppel to visit her husband for a few minutes alone.

Later, King Edward VII insisted on remaining dressed and in a chair. When he got up to talk to his two caged canaries by the window, he fell unconscious to the floor. He was undressed and put into his bed, where he flickered in and out of consciousness until he died peacefully shortly before midnight on 6 May 1910, surrounded by his family.

The new King, George V, wrote in his diary, 'I have lost my best friend and the best of fathers. I never had a [cross] word with him in my life.'

Death of a King, and an Archduke

Among the hundreds of letters received by George V over the following days, was one from the woman who had been the last to dine alone with his father, and who could flatter herself on being one of his dearest friends:

8th May

Sir,

With all my heart I am praying for help for you. I hardly dare think of your sorrow, & your responsibilities. Thousands & thousands of people are feeling the same, & that must be your comfort now. Just as we would have sacrificed everything for our beloved King, so we will be loyal to you, & work for you.

May God help you & bless you now & always.

Your devoted servant,

Sister Agnes[3]

The King's death affected Sister Agnes deeply, and Queen Alexandra, knowing how fond she had been of him, placed a spray of red roses from her on his coffin.

Edward VII was the first sovereign to lie in state in Westminster Hall in order that his people could pay their last respects. Seeking no priority in the queue, Sister Agnes stood in line and, conforming to the silence of the chamber, walked slowly past the body of her old friend, guarded by the gentlemen-at-arms at each corner, heads bowed.

Meanwhile, the monarchs and heads of state from Europe and beyond poured into London, packing Buckingham Palace and the city's great hotels.

On the day of the funeral, Sister Agnes travelled in the sovereign's group of carriages heading to Paddington station and thence to Windsor.

The streets were rich in purple [wrote the King's biographer], Venetian masts wreathed in laurel leaves bordered the funeral route. Houses, hotels, clubs and shops in the vicinity were fringed with purple or white. At Paddington even the girders and pillars of the platform were draped in funeral colours . . . the cavalcade was such as rarely if ever had been seen before or since . . . Blazing with orders, resplendent in the scarlet and gold and blue and silver of military uniforms, came the kings and a vast number of princes and nobles . . .[4]

The real star of this magnificent parade was Caesar, King Edward's devoted fox terrier which, since his master's death, had been haunting the corridors of Buckingham Palace in fruitless search for him. Now, led by a Highland servant, he followed behind the coffin. No one was more touched by this sight than Sister Agnes. Her little dog Needle had played so often with Caesar.

At the Chapel Royal at Windsor, during the memorial service, Lord Burnham, an old friend of Sister Agnes, told this story:

Not very long before the King's death there lay in the good Sister's charge an officer who was very, very ill, after a serious operation, and who, it was thought, could not survive.

The King was coming to the hospital to pay one of his quiet visits, and the patient, who heard he was expected, and was almost too weak to speak, said it would be a great happiness to him if he could hear his voice, and he asked Sister Agnes if it would be possible for her to talk to King Edward outside the open door. Sister Agnes said she would try to do what he wished, and, having in due course led the King there, she told him what her purpose had been. In a moment he went through the open door to the bedside of the ill man, and taking his hand held it for a long time, whilst he spoke to him words of tenderness and sweet counsel, and, when he had finally said goodbye, he slowly walked to the window and looked out upon – well, he looked out upon nothing, as the tears rolled down his cheeks, and then silently left the bedside of the sufferer whose strong desire it had been to listen to his voice . . . This picture which I have ventured to present to you is not a picture of the great King surrounded by all the pomp and circumstance of his State and splendour; it is the simple picture of a man with a tender heart impelled by his gentle and sympathetic nature to try and bring some solace, some comfort be it ever so little, to one who had fallen on evil days, but who in the past so far as in him lay had doubtless done his best in the service of his country and his sovereign.[5]

After the funeral and the departure of all the royal families, heads of state and foreign dignitaries, life in the capital began adjusting to the new reign. As far as the Hospital was concerned, there was little to do. There was real affection between King George and Queen Mary, and Sister Agnes. The King now became Patron, and continued his keen interest in the activities at the Hospital. There are a number of entries about it in his diary: 'May [sic] & I went to King Edward Hospital for Officers where Sister Agnes showed us round & we saw all the Patients.'[6] At the same time, it was inevitable that a measure of the old intimacy between sovereign and Sister had been lost with the death of King Edward, as Sister Agnes had anticipated.

One thing that the new King did appreciate was the ever-present concern about the finances of the Hospital. To run a charity hospital for officers in time of war and crisis was one thing; to maintain the contributions year after year in times of peace was quite another. Sister Agnes and her family continued to pump money into the bottomless coffers of the Hospital, but even the Keyser family had some limit to their resources. Paying the wages of nurses, cleaners and cooks, and maintaining the big old building, demanded considerable resources annually. In 1910–12, the situation was not critical, but there was cause for concern, and it was with regret that Sister Agnes proposed that in future officers should be charged a nominal two shillings and sixpence a day towards their keep.

Once more, the South African interest came to the Hospital's rescue. In May 1912, Julius Wernher, whose generous donation in 1904 on behalf of Wernher, Beit had saved it from its financial straits, died. His estate was estimated provisionally to be worth £11.5 million, more than that of any of those other Randlords who had made fortunes out of South African gold and diamonds. The chief beneficiary was his son Harold, whose association with the Hospital was to prove critical to its continuing success.

The will was immensely long and complicated, but what became clear was that one of the biggest legacies was in favour of 'Sister

Agnes's King Edward VII's Hospital . . . having been left £25,000 with a share of the residuary estate, reckoned a year later to reach a possible total of £465,000'.*

This dramatic change in the finances of King Edward VII's Hospital could not have been more timely, and it was certainly an immense relief to Sister Agnes. A European war to dwarf all its predecessors increasingly threatened, and when it came, with all the newly invented weapons of mass destruction, it would lead to casualties on an unprecedented scale.

The sensitive and dangerous state of relations between the European powers was made all too apparent in 1913, on the occasion of the marriage of the German Kaiser Wilhelm's only daughter to the Duke of Brunswick. Tsar Nicholas II of Russia and King George V had come to Berlin for the wedding at the invitation of the Kaiser, but he at once showed his jealousy of the friendly nature of relations between the British and Russian monarchs, and did all that he could to keep them apart. 'Fritz' Ponsonby recalls a particular luncheon:

> The Emperor kept off any delicate questions with the King, but when he sat next to Bigge [Arthur Bigge, private secretary] at the luncheon given by the officers, he let drive freely. He said that it hurt him very much to find we had agreed to send a hundred thousand men to help the French against him. 'I don't care a fig for your hundred thousand. There you are making alliances with a decadent nation like France and a semi-barbarous nation like Russia and opposing us, the true upholders of progress and liberty.'[7]

The spark which lit the fuse that led to the explosion of war between the central powers (Germany and Austro-Hungary) and the western allies (Belgium, France and Great Britain and her Empire) occurred at Sarajevo, Serbia, just a year after that wedding in Germany. It has often been described, but never better than by the late George Malcolm Thomson:

---

* The purchasing power of the pound sterling was at least fifty times more in 1914 than it is today.

The Archduke Franz Ferdinand was making a military visit to Bosnia in his capacity as commander-in-chief of the Austrian army. He and his wife drove into the town in the second of four motor-cars. Opposite them sat the Governor of Bosnia, Oskar Potiorek. In front with the driver was Count Harrach, head of the motor corps. As they came near the city hall the crowds were dense and the popular welcome was gratifying if not enthusiastic. At half past ten something struck the hood of the car behind the royal pair. It fell into the road, and exploded when the third car passed. Two officers of the Archduke's suite were wounded, one of them seriously. The Archduke ordered his car to stop. Meanwhile, the man who had thrown the bomb fled over the bridge that spans the river at that point. He was caught by the police. He turned out to be a young compositor named Cabrinovitch.

'So you welcome your guests with bombs!' exclaimed the Archduke furiously. As best he could, the burgomaster made his speech of welcome. The imperial and royal guest recovered his composure sufficiently to reply, reading in his thin, high-pitched voice from a manuscript spattered with his aide-de-camp's blood. Then he announced that he would go alone to the hospital to visit the wounded officer. His wife, however, insisted on going with him: if there was danger that was only the better reason why she should be at his side.

When Count Harrach said he was astonished to discover that there was no military guard to protect the heir to the throne, Potiorek sneered, 'Do you think Sarajevo is full of assassins?' There were only 120 policemen in the town and no soldiers, although two Austrian army corps were in the neighbourhood.

The four cars drove off once more, faster than before and along a route different from that which had been announced. Count Harrach stood on the running-board of the Archduke's car, a drawn sword in his hand. There were few police about. By a mistake, the first car turned into Franz Josef Strasse, which had been on the original route. The Archduke's driver was about to follow when Potiorek corrected him, so that the car went forward at a slow pace along the riverside quay. Two shots were fired from a distance of less than ten feet.

Sarajevo was full of assassins.

Potiorek excitedly ordered the driver to find another bridge over the river. Only then did he realize that blood was gushing from the

Archduke's mouth over his green uniform. His wife was leaning on him, unconscious but with no visible wound. 'Sophie, Sophie, live for our children,' gasped the Archduke. They were carried to a room in the Koniak (the government building) next to one in which the champagne was cooling for lunch. A quarter of an hour later both were dead.

The murderer was seized by the crowd. He had taken cyanide but his body had rejected it. He was a Serb student, an Austrian subject, named Gabriel Princip.[8]

CHAPTER 4

Armageddon

NEVER WAS THE decision by King Edward VII to persuade Sister Agnes to keep 'their' Hospital open in peacetime better justified than at the outbreak of war in August 1914. The assassination in Sarajevo led to a crisis between Austria and Serbia which intensified with every effort by the Serbs to placate the anger of the Austrians.

In Britain it had been a quiet and peaceful summer. There was the usual July holiday exodus to the seaside. The weather was warm and dry. Even the First Lord of the Admiralty, Winston Churchill, had stolen a brief break from the anxious scene in London. 'I went down to the beach,' he wrote later, 'and played with the children. We dammed the little rivulets which trickled down to the sea as the tide went out. It was a very beautiful day. The North Sea shone and sparkled to a far horizon.'[1]

Then, suddenly, to international dismay, and after the rejection of every peace proposal, Austria–Hungary declared war on Serbia. Far-seeing diplomats had predicted for years that 'trouble in the Balkans' would ignite the flames of a great European war. And so it happened. The fire spread with terrifying speed. The Russians mobilized against the threat of invasion by Austria, and Germany declared war on Russia. France mobilized to the aid of her ally. Three days later Germany declared war on France as well and invaded Belgium. Britain in turn declared war on Germany on 4 August.

The size of the hosts marching to battle was colossal. They mustered 335 infantry divisions – say, from five to five and a half million men. Add about fifty cavalry divisions, corps and army troops and odds and ends, to bring the figure to well over six million . . . Naval strengths amounted to at least half a million men . . . The biggest army was the Russian, with 114 infantry divisions. The French mustered sixty-two divisions . . . Germany put into the field eighty-seven divisions . . . Austria forty-nine divisions. The British would have been the best of the lot if there had been enough of them. Military critics talk airily of the superiority of small professional *armées d'élite* over 'armed conscript hordes'. Very good; but in the first place the main enemy [Germany] had a magnificent army, and in the second, small armies feel losses more sharply than big . . . To begin with Britain could send to France only the expeditionary force of six divisions.[2]

These British divisions became known as 'the Old Contemptibles'. They gained their derisory name from an order supposedly issued by Kaiser Wilhelm on 19 August 1914: 'It is my royal and imperial command that you exterminate the treacherous English, and walk over [their] contemptible little army.'

On that same day, Sister Agnes issued this formal announcement: 'I have enlarged this hospital and am quite READY for ANY NUMBER of SICK AND WOUNDED officers. There is nothing to pay and all officers are eligible.'

'Any number' was a somewhat extravagant claim when she had sixteen beds in all, and particularly considering the number of wounded in the first weeks of war. But Sister Agnes had further plans for expansion, as we shall see. At the same time, and with the full approval and support of her Patron, King George V, she was ready with a powerful team of doctors and surgeons at the outset of the conflagration, fully up to date with the numerous important advances in medicine since the Boer War, just as the Chief of the General Staff and the War Council appointed the most worthy and meritorious generals and admirals to the senior commands of the fighting services.

From the beginning it was made clear that patients at 9 Grosvenor Gardens might 'if desired be treated by any member of the Surgical Staff of a London Hospital'. In the event, this choice was rarely exercised, as the appointed honorary staff were of such a high calibre.

None of these specialist men of medicine was paid a penny for treating the wounded throughout the war. Such was Sister Agnes's reputation that their own reputation was enhanced beyond the value of any fee. To work for the sovereign and Sister Agnes was sufficient, indeed a privilege. At the same time, all the appointed honorary staff were free to practise in a private capacity.

This is the list as drawn up by Sister Agnes a few days before the war:

Dr W. Hale White MD FRCP
Sir Bertrand Dawson KCVO MD FRCP
Sir William Bennett KCVO FRCS
Sir William Arbuthnot Lane Bt. CB MS FRCS
Mr Herbert J. Paterson MC FRCS
Mr J. P. Lockhart-Mummery FRCS
Mr James Sherren FRCS
Mr T. Crisp English FRCS
Mr Charles Morris CVO FRCS
Dr Harold Spitta MVO MD
Dr Joseph Blomfield MD
Mr E. W. Clapham
Mr Arthur H. Cheatle FRCS
Mr Richard R. Cruise FRCS
Mr W. H. Clayton-Greene FRCS
Mr F. M. Farmer LDS RCS
Dr Theodore Thompson MD FRCP
Dr E. Farquar Buzzard MD FRCP
Mr Thomas Walker FRCS
Mr Llewelyn Powell
Mr Arnold Lawson
Sir G. Lenthal Cheatle KCB CVO FRCS
Mr John Thomson-Walker FRCS

Several of these consultants are worth singling out. William Hale White, for example, of Wimpole Street and Guy's Hospital, was appointed for his specialized knowledge of the liver and colon – he had written books on both, and numerous articles for the top medical journals. He was fifty-seven years of age when appointed at the outset of the war.

John Lockhart-Mummery, known colloquially as 'King Rectum', specialized in diseases of and surgery in that area. He had done much work on cancer of the colon, rectum and anus, but in terms of wartime surgery, Lockhart-Mummery was concerned with gunshot and shell splinter damage of the same area. He was only thirty-nine years old when the war began, and was to be tireless in his work for Sister Agnes; by 1918 he had probably carried out more operations than any other surgeon at the Hospital. (He lived on into his eighties, and was being consulted almost to the end.)

Joseph Blomfield was the complete anaesthetist, who assisted at hundreds of Sister Agnes's operations. The *Lancet* published his learned articles on his subject. At a time of rapid development in anaesthetics, Blomfield became Chairman of the Anaesthetics Committee of the Medical Research Council and Royal Society of Medicine. He also became President of the Association of Anaesthetists and editor of the *British Journal of Anaesthesia*.

The surgeon with whom Blomfield worked more than any other was James Sherren, specialist in abdominal surgery and surgery of the peripheral nerves, and author of numerous articles on the subject. It is doubtful whether he kept count of the number of bullets and fragments of shell he removed from the abdominal area of unfortunate officers, many of whom owed their lives to his skill and experience, but had he done so it would have been a remarkable total. During the war years he must almost have lived at 9 Grosvenor Gardens.

The Royal Navy representative on Sister Agnes's staff was Surgeon-Admiral George Cheatle KCB CVO, who had served earlier in South Africa and was four times mentioned in dispatches. He was a King's College man, and became one of that institution's consulting surgeons and its Emeritus Professor of Surgery. His portrait shows a good-looking surgeon–sailor, and hints at the cheerful and intelligent nature which made him a certain favourite of Sister Agnes. She appreciated natural charm as well as a title.

Her main ophthalmic man was Arnold Lawson, aged forty-seven, whose father had been surgeon–oculist to the late Queen Victoria. The Queen had always feared blindness inherited from George III, and Lawson (Sen.) was kept busy by her in her later years. The son was appointed Hon. Surgeon to HM King George V. Lawson was also editor and part-author of the standard work, *Lawson's Diseases of the Eye*.

The Hospital's urologist was John Thomson-Walker, a Scotsman, medallist in chemistry and physiology, and prizeman in gynaecology and medicine at Edinburgh. Thomson-Walker had recently published papers on surgical diseases and injuries of the genito–urinary organs, and was called in as consultant for wounds in this area. He was knighted for his services after the war.

Soon after the opening of hostilities, it became evident that the mouth and teeth were especially vulnerable to gunshot wounds. This had been the case in South Africa as well, and Sister Agnes had the foresight to appoint two dentists. The more eminent was Francis Farmer, knighted in 1916. He was, like several other of Sister Agnes's consultants, a London Hospital man, and no greater credit can be given to his work at 9 Grosvenor Gardens than the standard work which he later wrote with the cheerful title, *Restoration of Chin after Gunshot Wounds*.

For tricky bone operations, in particular, Sister Agnes could confidently rely on Sir William Arbuthnot Lane, a Scotsman of fifty-eight years of age who had been awarded his baronetcy just before the war for his work as consulting surgeon to Guy's Hospital and to the Hospital for Sick Children, Great Ormond Street. His best-known books were *Manual of Operative Surgery* and *Diseases of the Joints*. He later became known as the top man on surgery of cleft palates.

Mr Crisp English worked hard and often at 9 Grosvenor Gardens at the beginning of the war. He had been consulting surgeon to a number of hospitals, and the medical officer in charge of the troops at the Tower of London. After a year with Sister Agnes, much to her regret, he felt he wanted to be nearer to the war, and became an operating surgeon in France. Then he was appointed consulting surgeon to the Salonika force, and finally to British forces in Italy. He was mentioned in dispatches four times, and appointed KCMG in 1918 for his fine work.

In the relatively small world of medicine in London at that time, Sister Agnes's honorary consultants mostly knew one another, some better than others. E. Farquar Buzzard, a distinguished neurologist, and later President of the Association of British Neurologists, was more likely than most to be met on the steps of 9 Grosvenor Gardens, going in or out. When the fighting was over, Buzzard was appointed KCVO, and was later raised to the baronetcy.

Sister Agnes admitted her first seventeen wounded on arrival from France and Belgium just eleven days after the Kaiser had issued his famous order to wipe out the British Army. The soldiers' performance had been far from contemptible. Indeed the German infantry were deceived into believing that every British soldier was equipped with a machine-gun, such was their rate of fire with their Lee-Enfield rifles.

All Sister Agnes's 'young men' had been struck down in the Cambrai area where the British, greatly outnumbered, were putting up a stout resistance to the advancing German armies west of Amiens. Among them was the French-sounding Captain D'Esterre of the East Lancashire regiment, with four bullets in his right arm and hand; and Captain Francis Grenfell of the 9th Lancers who also had arm and hand wounds. In the retreat from Le Cateau his cavalry squadron had succeeded in saving the guns of a battery of field artillery in the face of ferocious enemy fire.

The Prime Minister Herbert Asquith wrote, 'It is on occasions like this that good discipline tells. The men were so wonderful and so steady that words fail me to say what I think of them, and how much is due to the colonel for the high standard to which he has raised this magnificent regiment.'

Grenfell's own words on the subject were: 'My fingers were nastily gashed . . . a piece of shrapnel had taken a piece out of my thigh; I had a bullet through my boot and another through my sleeve; my horse had also been shot, so no one can say I had an idle day.'

Captain Grenfell was awarded one of the first VCs of the war for his part in this action. He rejoined his squadron, and three weeks later suffered a thigh wound at Messines. He recovered from this serious wound only to be killed at Hooge on 24 May 1915. His brother Riversdale had also been killed in action earlier. These young men were both cousins of the Hon. Stephen Grenfell, who was himself killed in 1915, and sons of Lord Desborough.[3]

The distribution process of wounded officers with a 'blighty'* increased in efficiency as the numbers rose. Early in the war, officers were assigned to hospitals on arrival at the London railway terminals serving the Channel ports. But sometimes Sister Agnes heard directly from wounded officers abroad, anxious to come under her care when they arrived back in England.

One of these was Lieutenant John Lloyd Rennie of the Black Watch who had been wounded at Ypres by a rifle bullet which had gone through his lower leg, smashing his tibia. He had been treated at Boulogne hospital, where the rapid formation of pus in his leg had necessitated many incisions. Here he also heard about King Edward VII's Hospital and wrote to Sister Agnes early in December 1914. Sister Agnes replied, in a handwritten letter, on 7 December:

> I shall be very glad to have you here. You must tell General Donovan at Southampton & Captain Brand (who meets the train in London) that you want to come here, & that I have promised to take you in here. Then it will be all right.
>
> I hope you are much better.
>
> Yours sincerely,
>
> Sister Agnes

According to the Hospital's records, the Lieutenant was admitted on 19 December, and after being treated by Mr Lockhart-Mummery, was discharged on 25 February 1915 for convalescence at 4 King's Gardens, Brighton.

The Captain Brand referred to by Sister Agnes was an officer keen for action but who was refused active service because he was too old. His formal title was Assistant Director, Medical Services (London District). His daughter later wrote of him:

> Because my father was on duty all day and many nights, my mother and I made a practice of lunching with him in a Whitehall restaurant on Sundays, and afterwards walking through the park and calling in on Sister

---

* A blighty was a wound that was bad enough for the victim to be sent home (i.e. to Blighty) for treatment.

Agnes and Miss Fanny Keyser. My father greatly admired them both, and their work, but especially Sister Fanny who kept the hospital running smoothly.

One of the earliest patients Brand assigned to Sister Agnes was Lieutenant V. A. G. Cecil of the 1st Hampshire Regiment, whose medical report read:

Wounded at Ligny 26 August 1914
Severe penetrating wound on outer side of right shoulder. Small entrance wound behind shoulder. Large exit wound front of shoulder exposing fibres of deltoid muscle. Pus oozing for first 36 hours.

A week later he was reported as healing well, and a few days after that he was discharged and went to his home in Hatfield, though he had to come up to London daily for wound dressing.

None of the wounds suffered by this first intake was life threatening and as pressure for beds was heavy, patients were sent to a convalescent home or to their own homes after a few days. Major Herbert Blakeney was an exception. At forty-three, he was Sister Agnes's oldest patient so far, and he had certainly seen the most service, having fought for two years in South Africa where he was twice mentioned in dispatches and awarded the DSO. In France he had been at the retreat from Mons when he was hit by a rifle bullet in the chest to the left of the mid-dorsal spine; it broke several ribs and, as was common, left behind it a large, ragged exit wound. The Major suffered haemoptysis (the spitting of blood from the lower air passages) after the wounding, and had to be 'kept quiet under observation'. He was eventually sent to Osborne to recuperate, after which he returned to the Western Front. He survived the war and was awarded the Companion of the Order of St Michael and St George (CMG) in 1918.

The Irish Guards were in the heat of the fighting that autumn and winter. The first officer of this regiment, Lieutenant the Hon. Hugh Gough, arrived at 9 Grosvenor Gardens on 1 October, having been wounded two weeks earlier at Souppière. A bullet wound in the forearm had become gangrenous and an officer of the Royal Army

Medical Corps (RAMC) had amputated the arm below the elbow. By the time Gough reached Sister Agnes he was described as 'much troubled with pains and feelings in the absent hand and fingers'. He was also found to have a superficial wound, and under gas a fragment of metal was removed. This twenty-two-year-old, whose mother was a Pakenham, his father a 3rd Viscount, insisted on going back to the front, where he earned an MC and was twice mentioned in dispatches. He survived the war.

A second officer from this regiment who was warmly welcomed by Sister Agnes on 4 December 1914, especially as he was heir to the Earldom of Kenmare, was a twenty-three-year-old known as Valentine, more formally as 2nd Lieutenant Viscount Castlerosse. He had picked up a bullet in an elbow at Villiers Cottérêts, and was operated on at 9 Grosvenor Gardens by Mr English, who removed some bone, bringing back limited movement to the joint. Unlike a younger brother, killed a few months later, he returned to his regiment and survived the war. Valentine later became a considerable figure around the London West End clubs and in Fleet Street where he was a crony and fellow director of Lord Beaverbrook. Castlerosse was a man of much charm although his weekly gossip column was feared by some.

There are several entries whose subject was first 'completely healed, gone out again' and then, mournfully, 'wounded again, died'. One of these referred to an Irish Guards officer whose first wound was treated at 9 Grosvenor Gardens. He had been hit by a Mauser bullet on his sword blade and scabbard which, far from protecting him, led to his thigh being filled with 'numerous metal fragments'.

When the number of wounded from France grew out of hand – seventy-one were admitted in one early week of the war – Sister Agnes appealed to neighbours in Belgravia to help out. Generous-minded people cleared bedrooms for patients and nurses, and they and their servants, who necessarily had to work longer hours, made various other sacrifices.

Mr Pandeli Ralli, an immensely rich one-time MP who lived at 17 Belgrave Square, was one of those who offered his entire house and the use of servants. Captain Grenfell was transferred to this address when he had sufficiently recovered from his operation.

Others who rallied to the cause were the wife of the banker and chairman of the *Yorkshire Post* Sir Walpole Greenwell, a landowner and breeder of pedigree stock, who had served in the South African war. There developed a steady traffic of ambulances about Belgravia, from one smart residence to another.

King George maintained a great interest in all this activity taking place outside 'the back door' of Buckingham Palace, and on 1 October, by which time the satellite mini-hospitals were well organized, the King, accompanied by Queen Mary, made a round of visits to the patients.

Later, Queen Mary conceived the idea of giving convalescent officers tea in Buckingham Palace gardens. Sister Agnes always led these parties, crossing the road at the bottom of Grosvenor Gardens. One can picture the minute figure in immaculate white uniform leading her party across the road in front of the pedestrians and those on or in omnibuses.

Commander Michael St John RN recalls his father telling of one of these visits:

> One day my father was wheeled in on a chair and lined up with half a dozen others to be presented. Wounded officers in those days wore civilian clothes – the inevitable Marlborough jacket and bowler – and as the couple came down the line shaking hands, my father with difficulty got himself standing with the aid of two sticks, putting his bowler on the seat behind so as to have a hand free. Seeing how frail he was the King told him to sit down, and in his relief, my father forgot about his hat and started to subside gratefully into his wheelchair. Queen Mary, close behind the Monarch and spotting the impending disaster, leapt forward and with her rapier-sharp parasol, made as if to knock the bowler out of harm's way, but instead succeeded in impaling it like a brochette and waving it aloft to everyone's huge delight – Sister Agnes's and King George's in particular . . .

As the pressure on the Old Contemptibles increased in Flanders and France, so the numbers of casualties increased and with them, the pressure on Sister Agnes's resources. The staff of doctors and surgeons more than doubled. They all worked on an honorary basis, but nevertheless the cost of running these house–hospitals grew enormously.

Sister Agnes started a Special War Fund, and in the heat of patriotism ruling at the time, the money came rolling in. Mr Ralli, besides underwriting all the costs of running his house, donated £1,000 in a lump sum. So did Lady Wernher, who similarly offered her enormous house in Hertfordshire, Luton Hoo, as a convalescent home. Her husband Harold, serving with the 12th Lancers, added his name. Members of the Jewish banking families and firms were especially prominent and generous, including Sir Ernest Cassel and Louis Bischoffsheim (who had helped him in his early days in London), and the firm Schroeders and Neumann. Others gave a lump sum, usually £250 (£12,500 in today's money) and a guarantee of so much a week for the duration of the war.

Although Sister Agnes undoubtedly preferred to have officers from the best regiments – the Household Cavalry and the Brigade of Guards for example – she also had a soft spot for those from the Dominions, who increasingly manned the trenches from 1915. One of these was Oscar Orr, who had been commissioned in the field after serving with his regiment as a private. Orr was of Irish descent, born in the Canadian North-West Territories in 1892. 'We young soldiers,' he wrote, 'had a common saying, that the life of a subaltern in the PBI [poor bloody infantry] was ninety days. I did not make it . . . At the "Bluff", Ypres salient, 16 July 1916 I caught a piece of 5.9-inch-high explosive between the eyes.'

He went on to describe the removal of the slug at a field clearing station, Remy siding, in Belgium:

It was the custom to ask the wounded where they would prefer to be sent. I was not asked. An officer came to me and said, 'Oh, Mr Orr you are for King Edward VII's Hospital.' I later found that my only civilian acquaintances in England, on hearing that I had been wounded, had made arrangements to have me taken to King Edward VII in order to be near their home . . . During my stay there I never saw a Canadian doctor.

We arrived at Charing Cross station, met by huge cheering crowds throwing flowers on our stretchers. It was the first day I had the bandages off my eyes and everything looked pretty wonderful to me. I was put in an ambulance with a major from the Irish Guards. We were unloaded at this big house and carried up a broad staircase.

At the head of the stairs was this lovely, tiny figure in a starched pale blue uniform with the ribbon of the RRC [Royal Red Cross]. She had marvellous hair and the smallest waist I ever saw on a lady of her size. She reminded me of a delicate Dresden china figurine. She was very obviously the boss and greeted us both kindly before assigning us to our beds. Except for her daily visit I saw very little of her. She scolded me once for setting my bandage on fire lighting a cigarette. She also gave me orders during a Zeppelin raid that I was to assist my [blind] neighbour to reach the basement if the raid got worse.

Everyone was very fond of Sister Agnes's sister, a bit old-fashioned, called Sister Fanny. She was a real dear. She did not wear a uniform and looked after the patients' recreations, games, books, papers, and the odd letter. I think she was also in charge of the key to the garden gate into the Buckingham Palace grounds, to which the walking patients were permitted at certain times.

The care at King Edward VII's Hospital was excellent. The butler used to come round the wards before meals and take one's order for dinner. Liquor was available in any form by request.

When I was able to be moved, I received through the kindness of Sister Agnes an invitation to spend some time at Norfolk House, St James's Square. This was living it up indeed. My only complaint was that the wonderful dinner served to the Duke and his guests did not start until about 8.15 p.m.

Not all Sister Agnes's patients were so fortunate. Captain N. W. F. Bayes of the Gloucester Regiment was hit by a single rifle bullet shortly before Christmas 1914. It struck his left leg, passed through the patella and exited through the upper part of the calf, fracturing the fibula and chipping the tibia *en route*. Mr Sherren operated on this officer. At first it seemed fairly straightforward but cellulitis (inflammation of cellular tissue) developed and he died shortly afterwards.

CHAPTER 5

The Widening War

A S THE WEEKS passed, the British line on the Western Front stabilized into a salient around Ypres, Armentières and Neuve-Chapelle. The nature of the fighting was reflected in the injuries suffered. There were fewer multiple bullet wounds, particularly of the right arm, fewer bayonet wounds, but many more shell splinters, and the first cases of trench fever and frostbite of the legs.

After conquering most of Belgium, the German army was hellbent on reaching the Channel ports of Calais and Boulogne. The Belgians resorted to opening the sluice-gates of their canals and flooding vast areas with sea water. This succeeded in halting the German battalions, while in the south the British initiated what became known as the First Battle of Ypres, when open warfare ceased and henceforth the fighting was paralysed by entrenchments, barbed wire, and machine-gun and artillery emplacements.

One military historian vividly describes the establishment of this trench warfare in the first of four winters of the Great War:

Gradually the bits of trench, scratched in the ground, irrespective of tactical siting, wherever an advance had come to an end, were linked together, deepened, and when possible drained. Dug-outs which were at least splinter-proof appeared in them. Telephone cable in almost inextricable tangles ran along the sides. In front stretched curtains of barbed wire on wooden stakes . . . The opposing forces became well-nigh invisible to each other, though observers on high ground with fixed telescopes saw occasional movement in the enemy's lines . . . And from the Swiss frontier to the English Channel this long snake-like excavation was being photographed from aircraft and reproduced on maps on which the very latrines could be depicted.[1]

The casualties were horrific on both sides. The Old Contemptibles were literally decimated, and at Ypres alone fifty thousand British fell, killed or wounded. The German attackers lost twice that number. By the end of the year 1914 British territorial reservists and hastily trained volunteers were already in the line.

Lord Glentworth, son of the 4th Earl of Limerick, was in Sister Agnes's briefly in June 1915. Later, he transferred to the Royal Flying Corps as a pilot and survived until May 1918. The first pilot arrived at Sister Agnes's in March 1915, and was starkly described as having 'fallen in his aeroplane', receiving many injuries. His broken bones and cuts were dealt with by Mr English, and he was packed off to Claremont a week later.

Although they had met with fearsome casualties when they first encountered the German battalions in Flanders, the British Expeditionary Force had been transported by the Royal Navy across to France without the loss of a single man, an achievement of which the Navy was very proud. They had feared attack by high-speed torpedo boats, and the Dover Patrol (as it was to be known) was on twenty-four-hour watch, providing escorts for the passage.

U-boat attacks were also feared, and as a precaution against these a flying patrol was instituted. This was a novel and far-sighted move; and even more advanced was the use of the world's first aircraft carrier, the *Hermes*, originally built in the nineteenth century as a protected cruiser, and modified for its new role. A launching platform surrounded by railings from which her complement of three aircraft could be put into the air was devised. After completing their patrol, her aircraft headed for land, or, in the case of seaplanes or amphibians, landed on the water alongside and were hoisted on board.

How effective the *Hermes*'s operations were is not known, but before long, on 31 October 1914, she was hoist with her own petard and was torpedoed and sunk by a U-boat off Calais. Rescue boats were soon alongside and most of her company was saved. One of the officers dragged from the sea, badly wounded, was the ship's flight commander, Lieutenant F. G. Brodnibb. He was taken to Deal infirmary in Kent. There this pilot was examined under an anaesthetic, and the report reads, '5 ins of lower end of right femur protruding through a wound – wound prolonged to patella . . . Limb put up in splint . . .' None of these injuries would be expected to prove fatal, but the Lieutenant's life was feared for when he developed double pneumonia. He pulled round, however, and was judged fit enough to be moved to 9 Grosvenor Gardens after several weeks. By June 1915 he was transferred to Chequer's Court for convalescence.

Another patient who was under the care of Sister Agnes at the same time as her first naval airman was Major Edward Moulton-Barrett of the 2nd Northumberland Fusiliers. He was from an army family and had already earned the Distinguished Service Order (DSO) at Ypres, where he had also picked up a rifle bullet in his shoulder, breaking the humerus three inches from the shoulder joint. This was a very unpleasant injury, but the Major was safely in Osborne House two months after he was hit.

Captain A. J. Agius of the London Regiment, Royal Fusiliers, had been in the thick of the fighting since he arrived in the South of France from Malta. His regiment, along with the Northamptonshire and Worcestershire Regiments, was not only holding its line but pushing the Germans back; 2nd Lieutenant Conybeare of the 1st Battalion, Worcestershire regiment, recalled the scene:

The Germans came on in a great mass. Their officers were in front waving swords, then a great rabble behind followed by a fat old blighter on a horse. There was a most extraordinary hush for a few seconds as we held our fire while they closed in on us. Then, at last, we gave them the 'mad minute' of rapid fire. We brought them down in solid chunks. Down went the officers, the sergeant-majors and the old blighter on the horse. We counter-charged, and back the rabble went full tilt for their own trenches four hundred yards away.

This brutal fighting around Neuve-Chapelle led to frightful casualties on both sides. One officer of the Worcestershires, with the unhappy name of Slaughter, was brought into Sister Agnes's on 1 February with a smashed femur from a rifle bullet. Sir Arbuthnot Lane operated and three weeks later Slaughter was dispatched to Plymouth for convalescence.

Just as the change in the nature of the fighting meant a change in the predominating type of wound which the Hospital had to deal with, so Sister Agnes noted that for the same reason she was beginning to receive relatively few senior regular officers, who now tended to be based at headquarters behind the front lines. An exception, in May 1915, was Major Horace Somerville Sewell. He was hit in the left thigh by a small piece of shell casing. One imagines, in view of his sterling record later, that he fretted at being separated from his men of the 4th Dragoon Guards on account of such a minor injury. Mr Lockhart-Mummery operated promptly, removed the foreign matter, and two weeks later the Major was discharged. He returned to the front where he earned the DSO and bar and was also mentioned five times in dispatches: a singularly gallant officer.

The world was learning fast that war was no longer confined to the battlefields, nor were civilians safe from its ravages. Both on land and at sea all life was threatened. Although the U-boat campaign against (mainly British) shipping was at an early stage, the sinking of the great liner *Lusitania* with the loss of 1,198 lives, 128 of them American, provided another warning of what was to follow.

Winston Churchill, First Lord of the Admiralty, was as shocked as anyone when German battle cruisers steamed across the North Sea to attack English east coast ports:

> The bombardment of open towns was still new to us at that time . . .
> The War Map showed the German battle cruisers identified one by one within gunshot of the Yorkshire coast . . . And the great shells crashed into the little houses of Hartlepool and Scarborough, carrying their cruel message of pain and destruction to unsuspecting English homes.[2]

The German High Command introduced two new forms of offensive in the first half of 1915, both in the category of 'frightfulness' as popularly defined. The first was bombardment from the air by means of bomb-carrying airships, or Zeppelins. By as early as January two of these monsters had dropped twenty-five bombs between them on a number of different targets in England, causing several casualties. To the indignation of the Queen Mother, Queen Alexandra, one of them headed for Sandringham, where it was observed by Her Majesty circling the royal residence in the night sky. 'This is too bad,' she complained. 'Those beasts went straight to Sandringham, I suppose in the hopes of exterminating us . . .'[3]

More general outrage was caused when a Zeppelin reached London for the first time on the night of 31 May. In a foretaste of the Blitz of 1940, seven civilians were killed and thirty-five injured, but the political and moral effect was out of all proportion to the number of casualties. It was soon apparent that almost every corner of England was vulnerable to the Zeppelins, which flew so high that they were almost invulnerable to attack by fighters and gunfire.

On the Western Front in the spring of 1915 the fighting was dour and relentless. The British, supported now by Indian and Canadian troops, captured Neuve-Chapelle. Rumours soon began circulating that the German High Command were ready to launch their second new weapon, their second new 'frightfulness', and might resort to poison gas to break the deadlock. This was against international law but there were signs that the Germans were in earnest, and it became clear that there was to be no limit to the obscenity of modern warfare. There were unexplained clanking sounds from the German trenches. These sounds were in fact caused by the positioning of over three thousand enormous gas canisters for release of the gas. Then, several prisoners were taken who volunteered intelligence about the preparations: the numbers of the batteries and their positions.

Gas as a weapon was very haphazard, depending as it did on the vagaries of the wind. Moreover, initiating this weapon of horror was additionally dangerous for the Germans, as the prevailing winds were from the west and there was always the risk that the wind would back or veer and blow into their faces. To mitigate this risk, the German infantry briefed to follow up the release of gas were all equipped with gas masks.

22 April 1915 was warm and sunny. After long days of waiting the German order was at last given. Their position was north of Ypres, on the west of the salient defended by a mix of Canadians, French colonial troops – part of an Algerian division – and British infantry.

Then, at about five o'clock in the afternoon, the quiet along the salient was broken by an outburst of German artillery fire. At the same time a thick cloud of yellow–green smoke was seen to emerge from the German trenches and begin to sweep implacably towards the 48th Canadian Highlanders. At the last moment, like a tide of fate, the cloud was blown off course.

As they saw it approach, the soldiers' instinct was to lie as low as possible in the trenches. But this was where the chlorine gas lingered longest, with fatal results, suffocating its victims to death within minutes. In the words of one lance-corporal in the reserve trenches:

> [We] noticed volumes of dense yellow smoke rising up and coming towards the British trenches. We did not get the full effect of it, but what we did was enough for me. It makes the eyes smart and run. I became violently sick. By this time the din was awful – we were under a crossfire of rifles and shells, and had to lie flat in the trenches. The next thing I noticed was a horde [of French colonial soldiers] making for our trenches . . . some were armed, some unarmed. The poor devils were absolutely paralysed with fear . . .[4]

There were many more Algerians, as well as Canadians and British, who could not get away and choked to death. After weeks of failure to dent the Allied line, the Germans advanced a mile in less than an hour. The new weapon had proved its effectiveness. And worse was to follow: mustard gas.

Sister Agnes admitted increasing numbers of gassed officers. The condensed Case Book entries only hint at the condition of these wretched wounded. The notes about one officer read: 'Gassed, mustard gas, vomiting, conjunctivitis, eczema of genitals . . .'; about Major P. Crow of the Royal Fleet Auxiliary (RFA): 'Gassed, conjunctivitis and laryngitis, hoarseness . . .'; and about Captain K. H.

Stokes of the RAMC, admitted the same day: 'Gassed, mustard gas. Conjunctivitis, irritation of skin. Vomiting all next day, also catarrh of nose and some cough. Temporary suppression of urine . . .'

As the months passed after the first successful German gas offensive, the Allies realized that this weapon would have to be employed by their own armies. Even before the first German gas attack, Winston Churchill had ordered experiments with smoke-making equipment, for use particularly at sea (he was at the Admiralty at this time). The British used gas for the first time at the Battle of Loos in September 1915; the Germans replied with a new horror, phosgene gas shells against the French at Verdun in June 1916.

Poisonous gas was a weapon of attack, and the number of cases at the Hospital rose at the time of German offensives. The German 'do or die' push in the spring of 1918 brought Brigadier-General R. N. Bray of the Duke of Wellington Regiment under Sister Agnes's care. He had the usual symptoms of mustard gas affliction: constant vomiting, conjunctivitis, laryngitis and bronchitis. By this period in the war, the Germans were firing gas shells, of which Lieutenant G. Turner of the Royal Sussex Regiment was a victim: burns on the head and scrotum, etc. The damage to their lungs in particular affected the victims all their lives, which in many cases were greatly shortened.

Although thousands of soldiers on both sides were killed or incapacitated by gas, the high-explosive shell was usually the more serious arbiter of fighting on the Western Front. At times it seemed almost as if the whole continent of Europe was shaking from the effect of thousands of shell explosions, and the thunder of the guns could sometimes be heard in London, bringing the reality of war into every household, while women in the munitions factories worked long hours to feed the insatiable appetite of the guns. Another signal of a German offensive was the arrival in England a few days later of shell-shocked officers.*

---

* 'Shell-shock' was a convenient colloquial term of the time, which embraced a number of disorders, including depression and hysteria. It could also be described as a neurosis with hysterical symptoms. It is now recognized as an illness.

A twenty-four-year-old Scots Guards officer was welcomed by Sister Agnes on 16 October 1916 shaking with shell-shock and deafness. What these men needed was rest and quiet, but unfortunately one of the effects of shell-shock was to make its victim shout deliriously and often in protest at his condition. A major in the Royal Scots Fusiliers was described in the Hospital Case Book as being 'broken down with nervous debility' and 'very tremulous, incoherent and noisy'.

Often shell-shocked officers carried the physical wounds of battle as well. Major Gill of the 17th West Yorkshire regiment was struck down at Fleurbaix by a fragment of a rifle grenade. It lodged in his left temple, but he continued fighting and commanding his men for a further two hours before he collapsed unconscious, vomiting violently. His wound was dressed at the nearest casualty clearing station, and he was shipped home where he ended up in the hands of Mr Paterson at King Edward VII's Hospital. The piece of metal was removed. 'The wound healed but he is nervous,' the report continues, 'and sleeps badly. Tires easily.'

From quite early on in the fighting, RAMC officers under sustained shell fire had 'nerves much strained'. They also had neurasthenia (fatigue and anxiety) and suffered from tachycardia, or abnormally fast pulse rate. A complete rest at Osborne House was ordered in one case.

Cases of trench foot (similar to frostbite) and trench fever (a sort of typhus) were other guides to the nature of the fighting. At the Hospital, a nineteen-year-old lieutenant of the 11th Gloucesters was admitted with trench foot requiring a toe amputation, and 'all the other toes much deformed'. A captain in the Northamptonshire regiment was struck down with frostbite of both feet in the bitter cold of January 1915. It took time for the inflammation to subside, and when he was discharged he could only walk with his heels on the ground.

At first sight there appear to have been a disproportionate number of accidents involving horses. But, while the cavalry charge of the last century was now outdated, the horse remained the principal form of transport for the vast supplies required in the fighting – which supplies included the animals' own fodder. Throughout Britain there was a form of conscription for horses, to the distress of many farmers who were at the same time being adjured to increase food production. In France, the shellfire from both sides wrecked the agricultural drainage system built up over generations of farming.

Lieutenant Watkins's horse stepped on his foot, and Sir Arbuthnot Lane had to amputate a toe. Captain C. B. Jackson of the Yorkshire and Lancashire Machine-Gun Corps had a leg broken when a motor bicycle collided with the horse he was riding. Cellulitis set in and it was three weeks before he could be discharged. King George V was never completely out of pain for the rest of his life after he fell during a troop inspection and was rolled on by his horse. The same thing happened to the unfortunate Major McNalty, who fractured his right leg under similar circumstances, and at about the same age as the King.

Lieutenant-Colonel Buckle fell with his horse, badly lacerating his face. A few weeks later Lieutenant Krohn of the RFA fractured his tibia when his horse fell on his right knee.

In the early days of the war the role of the Royal Flying Corps had not properly been determined and their primitive flying machines were not treated seriously by the High Command. Then the first air cameras were delivered and were able successfully to photograph the German lines and beyond. Maps were made up from these photographs and, weather permitting, the RFC could anticipate German attacks with precision.

A further use for these flying machines, wheeling and turning among the black bursts of shell fire aimed at them from the ground, was 'spotting'. As a result of experiments carried out by enterprising officers, a system of spotting for the guns was devised, using Morse Code messages from flying machines at around three thousand feet. Lieutenant D. S. Lewis recalled:

We went out with three machines fitted with 300-watt Rouget wireless sets, run off the crankshaft, and receiving sets with Brown relays . . . At last we got our chance and made about the biggest success of the war. We do nothing but range, sending down the position of new targets and observing the shorts. The results are really magnificent . . . During a battle, every enemy battery that opens fire can be promptly dealt with and accurately ranged on . . . The 9.2-inch howitzer can generally hit a target with the first three shots . . .[5]

Later, air fighting became much more serious, and the spotting planes were attacked by German machines fitted with machine-guns. Control of the skies became important to the armies fighting in the mud of Flanders.

Like horsemen, wounded RFC pilots also tended to gravitate towards 9 Grosvenor Gardens, where they enjoyed a special welcome from Sister Agnes, their heroic role appealing to the romantic side of her nature. One of the first of these, who was shot down in the frantic air fighting of April 1917, was Lieutenant A. D. Finney; he suffered a fractured right femur, according to his entry, which had the added enigmatic note, 'fell out of aeroplane'. A number of other RFC casualties attracted the same curious phrase. Mr Sherren dealt with two more aviators at this time with machine-gun bullets in their right arms. Captain Whitworth was brought in after a crash which dislocated his left ankle and unfortunately Mr Sherren could not save his left foot.

Captain Sir John Eardley-Wilmot 4th Bt. had fought in the Boer War, and, as a captain in the Rifle Brigade, was wounded at Ploegsteert (or Plugstreet as the Army called it) in November 1914, when a bullet passed through the lower part of his thigh. Mr Sherren operated, removing many pieces of loose bone. This was not only a blighty, but put the Captain out of the war altogether. However, he lived for twenty-five years after the Second World War, to the ripe old age of eighty-eight.

Captain the Hon. Leonard Tyrwhitt was Chaplain of the 26 Field Ambulance. At fifty-one years of age, he was close enough to the front line to be hit by a Mauser bullet above his left knee. When Mr Lockhart-Mummery had finished with him, and his wound had healed, the Canon was sent to Claremont to convalesce. He had been Canon at St George's Chapel, Windsor, before the war, and was made Chaplain to the King. He died in 1921, heaped with honours and having been mentioned in dispatches for his war service.

Another well-born Guards officer welcomed by Sister Agnes was Colonel Percy Reid of the Irish Guards, who was knocked unconscious by the explosion of two shells close to where he was standing. He remained unconscious for some time, and was so badly concussed that he was sent home and thence to King Edward VII's.

*

Most of Sister Agnes's patients were in their twenties, some as young as seventeen, but occasionally she received veterans in their forties and even fifties. By chance one day in 1914, two officers in their forties were admitted. The younger of the two, Captain Singleton of the Highland Light Infantry, was from an army family. In fact, he had fought in South Africa at the same time as his father, who was killed at Majuba, while he himself was wounded at the siege of Mafeking and was afterwards awarded the DSO. Twelve years later, with nineteen and a half years' service behind him, he had the misfortune to be hit in the head with a shell splinter. After an X-ray, this was removed without any particular difficulty.

Lieutenant-Colonel Malony had a more troublesome head wound – and he was forty-seven years old. His entry reads:

Wounded Oct. 20:14 at Ypres. Rifle bullet Rt. temporal region. Bullet removed on field. Unconscious soon after injury. Operation at hospital Oct. 24:14. Bony fragments removed. Regained consciousness but had paralysis of leg, hand and face on left side. Hernia cerebri formed. This disappeared and the paralysis recovered first in the leg, next in the face but the arm still very weak. The opening in skull has fairly closed over.

Another forty-seven-year-old, Captain Rose, had an even rougher time, after being hit in the arm and head at the Battle of Loos, where he was made a prisoner of war. A German doctor amputated his left arm. Rose was exchanged for a similarly crippled German POW and was admitted to King Edward VII's in December 1916, where Mr Sherren found his legs in a dreadful condition, including septic arthritis of both feet. They had not the facilities to deal with all these problems, so he was sent in an ambulance to the orthopaedic hospital at Hammersmith. Here this elderly officer was relieved of his suffering by death under anaesthetic in April 1917.

On 25 November 1914, Winston Churchill, First Lord of the Admiralty, made a dramatic proposal at a meeting of the War Council. It was, no less, a plan to attack the Turkish Gallipoli peninsula, force a passage through the Dardanelles to Constantinople, enter the

Bosphorus and thus open a route to the Black Sea. This would virtually wipe Turkey out of the war, secure Egypt and the Suez Canal and
relieve the central powers' pressure on Russia, and at the same time it
would secure a line of relief to that ally for the delivery of much-
needed war supplies.

Turkey had entered the war on the side of Germany for many
reasons, not least because, thanks to a humiliating British blunder, the
two men-of-war of the German Mediterranean Fleet had been
allowed to escape the Royal Navy and reach Constantinople, where
they were presented as 'gifts' to the Turkish Government. This provided the Turkish Navy with some solace for the loss of two new
powerful Dreadnoughts, completed in Britain and commandeered at
the instruction of Churchill before they could sail to their rightful
owners in Turkey.

The Dardanelles campaign was a brilliant conception which went
cruelly wrong through poor leadership, weak planning and confusion
of interests, notably the reluctance of Lord Kitchener to divert any
troops from the Western Front, and Lord Fisher's reluctance to deprive
the Grand Fleet of any significant strength which was required for the
bombardment of the Turkish forts.

The Australian and New Zealand Army Corps (the ANZACS)
were almost on the spot, being trained in Egypt before their intended
embarkation for the Western Front. Instead, they were diverted to this
new enterprise. Brave as lions they were, but quite inexperienced. In
fact the whole attack was dependent on what was later called
Combined Operations. It had no modern precedent; the bloody
lessons were learned as the campaign proceeded.

The Australian Alan Moorehead summed up the Dardanelles campaign: 'It was the most imaginative conception of the war, and its
potential was almost beyond reckoning. It might even have been
regarded, as Rupert Brooke had hoped, as a turning point in history.'
Designed to break the deadlock on the Western Front, modern
weaponry led it to develop its own stalemate, with conditions just as
frightful as at Ypres and Verdun.

The experience of Captain Kenyon DSO after landing and seeking
a suitable site for artillery when it was brought ashore, was typical of
the confusion and the hellish risks undertaken:

The Colonel and I ran with the men to the top of the first hill, and then the Colonel stopped to look round, because of course our job was to reconnoitre for positions for the battery. Eventually he sent me off in one direction whilst he went in another. I rejoined him later and we both decided there was no place for the battery there . . . By then it was daylight and a gun from Gabe Tepe began enfilading straight down the beach. We walked in that direction keeping as far under the cliff as possible. There were a fair number of dead and wounded on the beach but no one moved the wounded. Everyone was too busy.[6]

Perhaps the worst moment in the whole campaign was the attempted landing from the ex-Channel ferry, *River Clyde*, on 13 June 1915, when the sea turned red from the blood of a thousand men who were blown to pieces by concealed Turkish machine-guns. Through the shattering gunfire, Colonel Williams recorded the futile dawn attempt:

6.25 a.m. Tows within a few yards of shore. Hell burst loose on them. One boat drifting to north, all killed.

Then ten minutes later:
Connection with shore very bad. Only single file possible and not one man in ten gets across. Lighters blocked with dead and wounded. Maxims in bows firing full blast, but nothing to be seen excepting a Maxim firing through a hole in the fort and a pom-pom near the skyline on our left front . . . Fire immediately concentrates on any attempt to land. The Turks' fire discipline is really wonderful. Fear we'll not land today.

Sister Agnes admitted the first wounded from the Dardanelles operation as early as 20 June 1915. Lieutenant Middleton of the RFA had suffered a gunshot wound in his left forearm. He had been first evacuated to Cairo where he was operated on and fragments of the bone were removed. He was operated on again on the hospital ship *en route* for home; the wound was opened and drained. When the unfortunate officer arrived at King Edward VII's Mr Sherren found it necessary to operate again, removing the tubes from the previous operation.

The Lieutenant at last healed well under the tender treatment of Sister Agnes and her nurses.

A month later the Hospital admitted a real veteran aged fifty years, Captain Robert Dundas Whigham, who had been shot in the right buttock at Gallipoli. He had served in the Nile Expedition in 1898, and fought at Atbara and Khartoum. This was followed almost immediately by service in South Africa where he was awarded the DSO. Mr Peterson removed the bullet and he was soon back in action. Whigham rose high in the Army, becoming Deputy Chief of the Imperial General Staff before the war was over.

Among an increasing flow of wounded returning to London from Gallipoli, several more followed Captain Whigham to 9 Grosvenor Gardens. One was the Adjutant to the 1/10 London Regiment, the Rifle Brigade, Captain the Hon. H. C. O'C. Prittie. Six weeks earlier he had been struck in the chest by a Turkish bullet which exited between the tenth and eleventh ribs. He was feverish with a high temperature and suffered from haemoptysis (the spitting of blood from the lower air passages) and a plueral effusion in the left side. This eventually subsided, however, and the Captain was discharged for convalescence.

Bombardments from the sea and further landings up the peninsula all failed to break the resistance of the Turkish Army. Not only did the fighting degenerate into trench warfare similar to that at the Western Front, but the Turkish soldiery were also mainly led by German officers, and armed with German weapons and ammunition. It was simply a longer journey home when you became a casualty. The conduct of the war was similarly unenterprising, with a lack of command, confidence and initiative. Time and again when an advantage had been attained, and at a heavy cost, there was a failure to follow through. Inevitably, the enemy counter-attacked and the advantage was lost. The series of Suvla Bay landings was a case in point. On the night of 6 August 1915 the 11th Division made a landing on the beaches of this bay on the extreme western point of the peninsula. 'Johnny Turk' was taken by surprise and there were few obstacles to overcome on the march inland. The ANZACs linked up with these new invaders, but instead of marching further, they were ordered to dig in. Meanwhile, the Turks concentrated new strength in the area, under the field command of Mustapha Kemal Atatürk, a fine general who later became President and reformer of Turkey.

Colonel Sir Maurice Hankey, on a tour of inspection for the Committee of Imperial Defence, went ashore with another officer and was appalled by what he saw:

A peaceful scene greeted us. Hardly any shells. No Turks. Very occasional musketry. Bathing parties round the shore. There really seemed to be no realisation of the overwhelming necessities for a rapid advance, of the tremendous issues depending on the next few hours. One staff officer told me how splendidly the troops were behaving, and showed me the position where they were entrenching! . . . I must say I was filled with dismay . . . What distressed me even more was the whole attitude of the division. The staff of the division and corps were settling themselves in dug-outs . . . It looked as though this accursed trench warfare had sunk so deep into our military system that all idea of the offensive had been killed.

'You seem to be making yourselves snug,' I said to a staff officer. 'Are you not going to get a move on?'

'We expect to be here a long time,' was his reply.[7]

With every day of entrenchment and passivity, the Turkish position strengthened and further Allied advance became increasingly unlikely. Theirs was a hopeless situation. At the same time the casualties mounted on both sides, and the numbers of wounded arriving in London after passage by hospital ship increased proportionately.

The first officer to arrive at 9 Grosvenor Gardens from this Suvla Bay enterprise was Lieutenant H. O. Dixon of the Buffs. A typical victim of trench warfare, as the fighting had become, Dixon had been struck by shrapnel. His wound was in the left shoulder, but the main fragment of steel had passed down the arm and lodged near the elbow. This fragment of shell was removed by Mr Paterson, and though a later X-ray revealed that some small pieces remained in his arm, it was decided to leave them *in situ* for the present.

Inevitably, the Dardanelles campaign was fizzling out for lack of planning, enterprise and determination – not of the men but of the command. Lord Kitchener himself visited the peninsula on 22

November 1915. He acted swiftly, dispatching home the commander-in-chief, and ordering an evacuation.

The withdrawal was the one part that was brilliantly, and secretly, managed. Not a man was lost. But what a futile exercise the campaign had been!

While the vast slogging match on the Western Front continued unabated, other campaigns were initiated besides the Dardanelles. The Mesopotamia campaign was concerned with the German–Turkish threat to India and the oilfields of Persia. While the ANZAC and British forces were landing at Gallipoli to the north, other British forces advanced against the Turks up the Euphrates valley from the Persian Gulf to Basra, Amara and, by September 1915, to Kut. But with the arrival of German officers, the campaign took on a new seriousness, and the British suffered a defeat at Kut. It took some months before Kut was retaken by the British, and Baghdad itself then fell in March 1917. The Arabs took advantage of these Turkish defeats and their guerrillas harassed the Turkish forces as they fell back on their homeland. They were also bombed and machine-gunned from the air.

This campaign led to the death of some 15,000 British troops in action, and as many from disease. About 50,000 were wounded. Sister Agnes was especially glad to welcome wounded officers from the more obscure campaigns. They gave the Hospital a more cosmopolitan tone. For example, the first to be admitted was Brigadier General C. C. Maynard DSO of the Devonshire Regiment, a senior professional officer with a remarkable record of soldiering behind him: the Burma campaign, the Tirah campaign, and the South African war for its entire duration. He had been awarded numerous medals and clasps. When it was decided to make a landing at Salonica in Greece in an attempt to come to the rescue of the Serbs, who were being beaten back by the combined forces of Bulgaria and Austro–Hungary, Maynard was among the first to land. The odds against the Franco–British force were too heavy, however, there was too much political bickering at home, and the Greek attitude to the campaign was too ambivalent, so it ended in failure.

The casualties among the Franco–British force were not unduly heavy, but they included Brigadier Maynard. Mr Sherren looked after him, and he was able to leave the Hospital after a mere two weeks.

Sister Agnes's first wounded officer from the Italian Front was admitted in March 1918. The British were no more than observers in the Italian–Austrian fighting, but Captain C. A. Cavendish of the 8th Yorkshire and Lancashire was unfortunate enough to be wounded in his right knee, arriving at King Edward VII's in March 1918.

By this time a new wave of weariness was beginning to overcome some of the staff. As always, they were braced up as far as possible by Sister Agnes, but she and her sister were far too sensible and practical to press the nursing staff – to say nothing of the consultants – beyond the point where their efficiency might be compromised. They decided to close the Hospital for a month.

The same thing had occurred in February 1916, when for five weeks the medical staff were granted leave and 9 Grosvenor Gardens was given a mighty spring-clean.

The last patients to be admitted before the closure of June 1918 included Lieutenant Sich of the Grenadier Guards, who had been in earlier but was still having trouble with a shrapnel wound in his right thigh; Lieutenant Tron of the 4th Hussars; Lieutenant Tilling of the 2nd Worcesters who had a fractured scapula from Passchendaele; Lieutenant S. C. Browning of the RFA; and Colonel Millward of the 11th Royal Sussex, who had a gunshot wound in his left leg. This had become infected before he reached London, and Mr Sherren had to amputate it.

Mr Cheatle had to carry out another amputation, on Lieutenant J. B. Roase, shortly before the Hospital closed. But all these officers were transferred safely to adjoining house–hospitals where they continued their recovery.

King Edward VII's reopened on 4 September 1918. By then, on the Western Front, the tide had really turned in the Allies' favour. The German people and the German armies alike were half-starved and demoralized. The German fleet was mutinous and refused orders to implement an all-out, last fling attack on the British Grand Fleet, while the German armies suffered crushing casualties. The newly arrived American First Army was fresh and eager for battle. The last days of September marked the beginning of the end. The combined armies of France, Britain and her Commonwealth, Belgium and the USA attacked on a wide front, liberating a vast area of northern France and Belgium, and the Channel ports including Ostende and Zeebrugge. Some half a million prisoners were taken and seven thousand guns captured within a few weeks. By mid-October it was clear that the central powers could never re-form. On 10 November the Kaiser fled to Holland, which had remained neutral throughout. On 11 November at 11.00 a.m. the German High Command met the Allies and signed a Treaty of Armistice.

The greatest war in history was over. The price in lives had been appalling, right up to the end.

Sister Agnes continued to admit the wounded long after the Armistice and the cessation of fighting. Major J. C. Hunter of the RFA, for one, was operated on by Sir Arbuthnot Lane for gun-shot and shrapnel wounds on 18 November. He was in a bad way and not helped in his recovery by severe neuralgia. Officers from the Grenadiers, the London Scottish, the Sherwood Foresters and other fine regiments were treated. Mr Lockhart-Mummery carried out two operations on the day the Armistice was signed. It was hard to have a bullet removed from your thigh, as Colonel Bamford did, or your small intestine, while the crowds in the street were celebrating the end of the war. At least, however, as they came round from their anaesthetic, Sister Agnes holding their hand as she had for all patients throughout the war, they knew that they would never return to the mud, the squalor, the pain, the fearful noise of the Western Front.

Quite quickly as the last days of 1918 ran out, the number of patients to 9 Grosvenor Gardens with war wounds declined, and the patients occupying the beds tended to be suffering from peacetime troubles, like haemorrhoids or infected appendices, but they were all military or naval.

Then, from March 1919, the Hospital felt the first effects of the world-wide pandemic of influenza which, in the course of a few months, killed more people than the total death toll of over four years of warfare: some 15–20 million.

*

Sister Agnes had numerous discussions with King George V, Patron of her Hospital, about its future, just as she had had with his father after the Boer War. This time there was no question of closing down now that the needs of war had been met. Its future function was clearly defined: King Edward VII's Hospital would continue to cater for the serving and retired officers of the armed services, and it could be assumed that there would be many whose wounds would continue to give them trouble. The number of admissions had risen to a total of over 7,000 since the first opening. When the King was given this figure he wrote this letter to Sister Agnes:

Dear 'Sister Agnes',

Grateful memories will remain in the hearts of many at home & overseas of 'King Edward VII's Hospital for Officers', of you, its founder, and the noble Medical Staff, whose eminent advice & unerring skill have brought to so many sufferers relief, comfort, & restoration to health.

It is to these Physicians & Surgeons that I, as Patron of the Hospital, desire to express my deep appreciation of & lasting thanks for the valued services & precious time which, during these momentous years, they generously placed at the disposal of the Hospital.

Believe me, dear 'Sister Agnes'

Sincerely yours,

George R.I.

CHAPTER 6

Peace and Restoration

T HE FIRST YEAR of peace for just over four years was a time of renewal of all aspects of life, from faith in mankind after what had seemed like endless killing and destruction, political resolve and reconstruction, the recreation of family life, and much else.

A similar need to consider the future embraced Sister Agnes and her Hospital. No one had worked harder from 4 August 1914 to 11 November 1918 than she had, and although she was now sixty-six years old, her energy and dedication had not diminished in any way. There were none of the doubts about whether or not she should keep her Hospital open as there had been after the Boer War.

For the past fifteen years she had shared under one roof her Hospital and her home, but even before the end of hostilities she had learned that the lease of 16 Grosvenor Crescent, the house next door to her own one-time home at number 17, was available. She therefore set about in her own brisk, commanding way acquiring this lease and planned to move her Hospital back to its old quarters, returning the house to her concept of the ideal hospital – small, neat, personal, easily managed and maintained. To signify her and Fanny's privacy on the one hand, and immediate availability and accessibility on the other, she had a through door put in on the ground floor.

A bronze plaque on the wall of the entrance hall in Beaumont Street today completes the story. It reads:

PATRON
HIS MAJESTY THE KING
PRESIDENT
H.R.H. THE PRINCE OF WALES
VICE-PRESIDENT
H.R.H. THE DUKE OF CONNAUGHT
THIS HOSPITAL HAS BEEN REMOVED BACK TO 17
GROSVENOR CRESCENT FROM 9 GROSVENOR GARDENS
AND OPENED BY THE KING AND QUEEN ON JUNE 12th
1919. IT IS GIVEN BY SISTER AGNES IN MEMORY OF
KING EDWARD

The move and reopening of the Hospital attracted the attention of the Press:

King Edward's Hospital for Officers has a new and permanent home, which the King and Queen honoured with an informal opening last week. Miss Agnes Keyser has transformed her house in Grosvenor Crescent into a perfect model of a small hospital, and the splendid nursing and choice surroundings with which she has helped hundreds of officers during the Great War will continue to be available. The hospital is, it need hardly be said, most charmingly decorated and furnished, and some of the wards have in addition the interest of association for those who knew them as rooms in a private house where Edward VII was so frequent and cordial a guest. Few women have done as much for soldier–sufferers in the war as 'Sister Agnes' and 'Miss Fanny'. All officers who have enjoyed their kindness will wish them a long term of continued benevolence at No. 17.

If any name can be singled out, after Sister Agnes herself and the sovereign after whom the Hospital is named, then that name must be Wernher. It was Julius Wernher who had made it financially possible for the Hospital to remain open after the Boer War, with the support of his business partners Alfred Beit and Friedie Eckstein. Twice between the wars Julius Wernher had transferred large sums of money in cash or securities to keep the Hospital going, most recently by the terms of his will in 1912.

Now in 1922, ten years later, after the fearful expenses of the war during which no contributions had been canvassed, and the expense of the move back to Grosvenor Crescent, the Hospital coffers were low again. Julius Wernher had died on 22 May 1912, leaving three sons, Derrick who inherited the title but was feckless and was virtually disinherited by his father; Harold ('Hackie'), born in 1893; and Alexander born four years later. After making proper arrangements for his widow, Alice ('Birdie'), Julius's estate was worth around £11.5 million, with Harold as the main heir and owner of Luton Hoo.

By the outbreak of war in August 1914, the Wernher estate was still not entirely cleared up. Believing that he 'had no head for business', Harold chose the Army as a career. But with his father dead, Harold was without a sponsor and did not know how to set about finding one. He also knew how close his father had been to Sister Agnes, and how much he had supported her Hospital. He therefore went to see her. As he expected, she was sympathetic and businesslike. Within hours of his leaving, she had spoken to the King, and thus HM George V became Harold Wernher's sponsor for a commission. Within days he was kitted out as a cadet at Sandhurst; but before leaving London for this military college, he again called on Sister Agnes. 'Can I do something for you in gratitude?' he is reported as asking her. Her answer is not recorded, but it could have been, 'Bide your time, young man. But I'll remember your offer.'

Harold enjoyed the life at Sandhurst in 1914 immensely. He was experienced and good with horses, as he was to be all his life. He played as much polo as he could, and rode to hounds as frequently as he was allowed. His training complete, Harold was commissioned in the 12th Lancers, a famous cavalry regiment. At the outbreak of war, 'the 12th' was one of the first regiments to be sent to France; there Harold actually took part in a cavalry charge, one of the last on the Western Front. But, later, while Sister Agnes was admitting her first wounded officers, he switched to the Machine-Gun Corps, which seemed a more modern and effective way of killing the enemy. He was fighting around Béthune, and was twice mentioned in dispatches. The scenes of war filled him with horror. 'Our parapets are made of dead men,' he wrote, 'and we cannot dig down for fear of exhuming a corpse.'

Harold survived unwounded, but his beloved younger brother Alexander, who had joined the Welsh Guards straight from school, was killed.

While on leave in the early summer of 1917, Harold proposed marriage to Countess Anastasia ('Zia') Mikhailovna de Torby and was accepted. They were married very grandly in the Chapel Royal on 20 July, in the presence of the King and Queen. Henceforth Harold's wife was known as Lady Zia Wernher. Harold returned to the war, this time to the Italian Front.

The Wernhers quickly had a boy and a girl, in 1918 George Michael Alexander, and in 1919, Georgina. Later on, in 1925, another girl was born, Myra Alice.

Harold's serious interest in King Edward VII's Hospital manifested itself soon after the war when he returned to pay his debt to Sister Agnes. Harold, tall and strikingly handsome, got on well with women, and Sister Agnes, now in her late sixties, fell under his charm at once. In 1922 he set about organizing the raising of funds in order that the Hospital could continue its good work.

Sister Agnes had already made arrangements, with the authority of the Patron and President, to issue a statement and appeal directly to the armed services. Dated 1 January 1920, the text read:

During the war, of course, we did not ask for subscriptions, but in many cases they were continued by individuals and by some regiments. We have nursed just under 7,000 officers here, and have treated and looked after a very large number of out-patients regularly. I have just moved the hospital from No. 9 Grosvenor Gardens, to my own house, No. 17 Grosvenor Crescent, where my sister, Miss Keyser, and I took in some hundreds of officers during the Boer War. I have quite made up my mind that a hospital of this kind is a necessity, so I have spent a large sum of money in making No. 17 most comfortable, and absolutely up-to-date in every detail. Now I want some help from the officers themselves, and, unless I feel sure of their support and appreciation, I am afraid I should not care to go on. As in peace time everything is free, but the officers make their own arrangements with their surgeons.

It is difficult to suggest the best way to subscribe, and I am told that in the Navy it can only be done individually; but it would be an enormous advantage in every way, and save a great deal of work, if, where possible, the Army could subscribe regimentally. Will you all think it over, as I am anxious to make satisfactory arrangements for the future.

Sister Agnes

The result of this appeal appears to have been favourable, and the number of regular subscribers climbed over the following years and, indeed, right up to the start of the Second World War. With the further financial assistance of Harold Wernher and Sister Agnes herself the situation appeared to be secure for the foreseeable future. The Hospital remained busy in the aftermath of the war, most of the patients being officers who had been gravely wounded and had to return for further treatment.

One of the longest-serving Trustees, Sir Walpole Greenwell Bt., died in October 1919 at the age of seventy-two, and this made necessary the appointment of a new Trustee. An indenture was accordingly drawn up, and his son Bernard, an industrialist who lived nearby in Eaton Square, succeeded not only to the baronetcy but also to his father's place among the Trustees. At the same time Harold Wernher was also appointed to the Board of Trustees. It is significant that, with the advent of Harold Wernher among the Trustees, 'at the same time certain changes were made to the Schedule of the Trust funds'.

During the 1920s the relationship between the Royal Family and Sister Agnes remained as secure as ever. King George V, for all his taciturnity, manifested a real affection for the Hospital (and not only because 'it was my father's creation') as well as for Sister Agnes herself, who brought cheer and vivacity whenever she arrived at Balmoral or Sandringham. As for Queen Mary, that equally formidable 'May of Teck' was deeply fond and admiring of Sister Agnes. She even restrained herself from admiring too enthusiastically some of the choicest *objets d'art* displayed in the Keyser sisters' private quarters, one of her less attractive practices, on the occasions when she and George were conducting one of their frequent tours of the Hospital.

Sister Agnes kept up an unremitting pressure on the Army Council, the Admiralty, and now the Air Council through Air Chief Marshal

Sir Hugh Trenchard, reminding them of the Hospital's existence, and pressing them to encourage officers in need of her care to apply for admission. This is reflected in an Army Council Instruction issued by the War Office in 1924:

No. 35 Sick officers desirous of admission to King Edward VII's Hospital . . . to be granted sick leave.

Officers sick in quarters or in hospital who are desirous of admission to King Edward VII's Hospital . . . for treatment, will in all cases be granted sick leave of absence for the estimated period of their unfitness as laid down in para. 1488, King's Regulations . . .

There are plenty of people alive today who knew or were patients of Sister Agnes in the 1920s and 1930s. One and all emphasize both her kindness of heart and the firmness of her regime. An officer in the RAF remembers her when, as a boy of no more than twelve years old, he visited with his aunt to see his first cousin. 'At one point,' he recalls, 'she turned to me and said, "If you're ever knocked down by a taxi in London, just say take me to Sister Agnes's and we will look after you."'

A serving officer in the Royal Horse Guards (the Blues) suffered a fall in a steeplechase and was taken to Sister Agnes's:

Because of my condition, I was kept in complete darkness, with the blinds drawn and no lights allowed on . . .

One afternoon I received a visit from a girlfriend, who probably should not have been allowed to see me, but managed to do so.

She was sitting on my bed when the door opened and Sister Aggie strode in. The wretched girl was ordered out forthwith and I received a blistering rocket – far worse than any I received later in my military career.

Surgeons also felt the lash of Sister Agnes's tongue when they contravened regulations, and in their case, with the unspoken threat of losing their authority to operate in the Hospital along with all the attendant prestige, these occasional outbursts were more seriously felt. However, Sister Agnes was not one to bear a grudge and she would soon return to her cheerful, smiling, bustling self.

As to the rank of her patients, though this was certainly noted, it mattered much less than the quality of their regiment. A junior lieutenant-commander recalls being in a ward of four beds:

Next to me was a very nice and very brave young flight-lieutenant who had, I think, lost a leg and had other injuries due to a 'prang'.

Opposite me was an admiral who shall be nameless. Apparently when I was coming out of the anaesthetic, and not responsible, the airman said to me, 'You are using awful language and there is an admiral in the ward.'

My reply was, 'What, not another bloody admiral.'

The admiral wore a night-shirt and had not any pyjamas. He used to leave the room early in the morning in only his night-shirt. Sister Agnes came into the ward and said, 'Really, Admiral, you are not to go about in your night-shirt. The nurses are used to it, but it's the maids cleaning the stairs that I worry about.'

She was a very kind martinet, as long as her rules and orders were obeyed. I found her quite delightful, with a sense of humour and devotion to her patients, and their well-being and recovery. A very dear lady.

The spring of 1926 was a worrying time for Sister Agnes. Her sister Fanny, two years older than herself, was seventy-six and although she did not behave like an old woman, she had cancer and required nursing. By the beginning of May she was clearly weakening.

On the fourth of that month Britain was struck by a general strike. For the first day or two London was in a state of chaos, with no transport, no newspapers, no food distribution. Then volunteers were organized and skeleton services, even of trains, brought back some form of life. For Sister Agnes, it was an added concern. Under normal circumstances, she would have been among the first to volunteer, seething with righteous rage against the strikers – the 'slackers' as she called them – but now her sister's condition occupied all her mind and most of her time. Then, on 19 May, after the strike was over, Fanny died.

It was a devastating blow for Agnes. She and Fanny had lived together all their lives, separated only briefly for holidays or weekends, and for her life would never be the same again. For months the staff noted her melancholy demeanour, and the loss of the spring in her step. Fanny's funeral was widely reported. The first part took place at St Peter's Church, Eaton Square, a short distance from Grosvenor Crescent, after which her body was interred in the family vault at Old Stanmore Church, where she and all her family had worshipped in the old days.

A quarter of a century later a distinguished admiral, Sir W. A. Howard Kelly, who as a young commander had been a patient at 9 Grosvenor Gardens in 1907 and again in 1911, recalled Fanny in a last tribute before he himself died:

> While Sister Agnes held the hand of every patient as he was going off and coming round from the anaesthetic, and was the clinical head of the hospital, it was Miss Fanny who, as housekeeper, and favourite sister, was responsible for the comfort and well-being of patients, and as such is affectionately remembered.

Fanny was described by another as being 'of a milder temperament and a less masterful personality than Sister Agnes, and . . . much loved by the patients'. Fanny had always looked after the Hospital library and distributed packs of cards or games as required. She also helped a great deal on the administrative side, in which capacity she would be sorely missed.

Three years after Fanny's death, it became clear to the Trustees that consideration should be given to the future of the Hospital after Sister Agnes died or was unable to work at the rate she had so far enjoyed all her life. This was the special concern of Harold Wernher, who had by now been a Trustee for a number of years. The other Trustees at this time were Sister Agnes herself, Sir Bernard Greenwell Bt. and Captain R. N. Macdonald-Buchanan.

These Trustees, led by Harold Wernher as Honorary Secretary, hardened themselves to the measures necessary to secure the future of the Hospital. It was inconceivable from a personal point of view that it might have to be closed while Sister Agnes was still alive; from a practical point of view, its function was clearly as important at that time as it had ever been. Wernher and the other Trustees (excluding Sister Agnes herself) were fearful of the founder's response to the suggestion of any reduction in her control of all aspects of the running of King Edward VII's. But if, as was proposed, the Hospital were to be granted a Royal Charter of Incorporation, it would mean the end of her absolute control.

It was a tricky situation, and in the end Harold Wernher volunteered to make the first approach. We can imagine the scene in Sister Agnes's private office: the immensely tall military figure with his bristling moustache coming through the door, limping as always from a riding injury from many years ago; and the diminutive figure of the seventy-six-year-old woman rising from her desk to greet her old friend and supporter. Had she got wind of the reason for this visit? Not much went on at Number 17 that she did not know about. Be that as it may – and in actual fact Wernher thought that the whole thing was a surprise to her, not to say a shock – she took the proposal calmly and rationally, immediately recognizing its merits. She had no illusions about her advancing years, and she could not deny to herself that since Fanny's death, the burden of office had immensely increased. As for Wernher, he felt both relief and admiration for this remarkable woman.

'The other Trustees suggest that you would wish to have Bircham draw up the draft of the application for the Charter.'

'Yes, indeed. I will ask him round for a talk,' she replied.

Halsey Bircham was Sister Agnes's old friend and solicitor, senior partner of Bircham and Co., who had guided her personally, and her Hospital, through any turbulence or litigation since the Hospital began. She arranged for him to draw up this draft with her usual speed and efficiency. Then it was submitted to the King, who approved it.

It is not necessary to quote the full length of this Charter, but it opens formally thus:

GEORGE THE FIFTH by the GRACE OF GOD of the United Kingdom of Great Britain and Ireland, and of the British Dominions beyond the Sea, King, Defender of the Faith:-
To all to whom these presents shall come Greetings:-
Bernard Eyre Greenwell, Baronet, of 2 Finch Lane, London, E.C., Sir Samuel Ernest Palmer, Baronet, of 10 Grosvenor Crescent, London, S.W., Colonel Harold Augustus Wernher, of Someries House, Regents Park, N.W. and Captain Reginald Narcissus Macdonald-Buchanan, of

Lavington House, Petworth, Sussex, the Founder and the Trustees of King Edward VII's Hospital for Officers have by their humble Petition humbly represented (inter alia) as follows: [There follow clauses covering the origins and financial arrangements of the Hospital, then:]

That the Founder has hitherto had the general control and management of the Hospital subject to the advice and assistance of a House Committee.

That the lease of No. 17 Grosvenor Crescent where the Hospital is situated is vested in the Founder and the whole equipment of the Hospital has been found at her expense and her intention is if and when a Charter is granted to the Hospital to make over to the Incorporated Body as a free gift the Lease and the whole contents of the Hospital.

Sister Agnes was, then, effectively yielding to others the control of her Hospital, and the structure of the Hospital itself.

Under the heading 'Interpretation', these were among the definitions:

'The Hospital' means King Edward VII's Hospital for Officers Sister Agnes Founder.

'The Founder' means the said Agnes Keyser.

'The Council' means the Council and appointed as hereinafter provided . . . [and so on].

In 1930 the Hospital's Patron was HM King George V, 'who shall be entitled to be present and vote at any General Meeting'.

The Prince of Wales [later Edward VIII] 'shall be the first President of the Hospital under this Our Charter.'

'Field Marshal His Royal Highness The Duke of Connaught, the present Vice-President shall be the first Vice-President of the Hospital . . . shall, subject to the conditions hereinafter contained, continue during the pleasure of the Governors or until resignation.' [The Duke never resigned and remained in the post until his death in January 1942.]

Besides the old Trustees, there were new names on the Council, among them Major-General Sir Kenneth Wigram, a real fighting general if ever there was one from the march to Lhasa, Tibet, to the Western Front when he was made CB, CBE, and was awarded the

DSO; Air Chief Marshal Hugh Lord Trenchard, the 'father of the RAF', and several notable doctors, including John Lockhart-Mummery, who had served the Hospital so well during the 1914–18 war.

The Charter was signed on 21 August 1930 – and a new era for the Hospital opened. The first meeting of the Council took place, appropriately, on Armistice Day of that year. The King addressed a letter of congratulation to Sister Agnes:

> On the occasion of the First Meeting of the Council of King Edward VII's Hospital for Officers, since it received the Royal Charter, I have much pleasure, as Patron, in offering you, the Chairman, and the Members of the Council my hearty congratulations on this important day in the history of the Hospital. I assure you of my sympathy with and good wishes for its welfare and I earnestly hope that, under these new conditions, the wonderful work which the Hospital has already achieved may be carried forward with renewed vigour and success.
>
> George RI

In June of that same year, 1930, Harold Wernher was knighted. In the citation as KCVO his services as Honorary Secretary to King Edward VII's Hospital for Officers were mentioned. Shortly after the war Harold and Zia had bought a country house and estate, Thorpe Lubenham Hall near Market Harborough, in the centre of fine hunting country. There they employed twenty-six staff, and built a recreation hall for them. For his own indulgence, Harold also laid out an eighteen-hole golf course, and built an indoor tennis court. Zia enjoyed a lavish lifestyle, while Harold conducted much charity work in addition to being Chairman at King Edward VII's. To cite only one, he took on the arduous responsibility of Chairman of the House and Finance Committee at University College Hospital.

Among the Wernhers' friends were the Mountbattens. Lord Louis ('Dickie') and Edwina Mountbatten were almost as rich as the Wernhers, Edwina having inherited great wealth from Sir Ernest Cassel. The Mountbattens also indirectly led Harold into a business career. Dickie's elder sister Louise married Gustav Adolf, Crown Prince of Sweden, and Zia and Harold were guests at the wedding.

This led to an association with a man called Axel Wenner-Gren, who had founded the Electrolux firm in Sweden in 1913. This well-made vacuum cleaner was vastly successful and by 1920 was known worldwide. The London agency was on a small scale, however, and when Wenner-Gren expanded into refrigerators he decided the time had come to set up a factory in England. By chance, he knew another Swedish industrialist who had a ball-bearing factory in Luton. When Wenner-Gren consulted his friend about finance and a site for his factory, his fellow Swede was able to oblige him on both counts locally. Thus it was that Harold visited Sweden and on their second meeting took a great liking to the industrialist and to his products. The outcome was that Harold invested heavily in the company and was appointed Chairman of Electrolux UK. The formalities were completed on 1 February 1926, the company having a capital of £1 million. The factory was opened on 18 May 1927.

Never, surely, did a businessman leave such a grand home in the morning for his office a few miles distant. Although Electrolitis (as he renamed the firm) took up much of Harold's time, it led to no neglect of his charities, least of all King Edward VII's Hospital, and Sister Agnes herself, who loved hearing about this new activity of her Chairman. The Hospital, moreover, was fitted for the first time with refrigerators from Luton, and vacuum cleaners for every floor. As for Luton Hoo and their London house, Harold no longer had to put up with warm Martini cocktails there, something he loathed.

A young man to whom the Wernhers became particularly attached was their son Alex's great friend Prince Philip. The Prince, a member of the Greek Royal Family, had a somewhat haphazard family life. His mother became mentally unstable and the couple separated. His uncle Dickie and his elder brother George became more or less intermittent surrogate fathers to this handsome and highly intelligent boy. Philip enjoyed staying at Lubenham. He loved talking to Harold, whom he considered among the wisest men he had ever met. The affection and respect were returned in full measure.

On 20 January 1936 the people of Great Britain and her Empire lost their King, and the Hospital carrying his father's name lost its Patron.

King George V had been a good monarch who had reigned through the horrors of the Great War of 1914–18 and the economic crises of the 1920s and 1930s. He had been a worthy successor to his father, Edward VII, and his grandmother, Queen Victoria.

It was George V who had initiated the practice of speaking to his people over the wireless on Christmas afternoon. On that day the previous month, his broadcast gave the first hint to his people that his health was declining, as described by his biographer Kenneth Rose:

His Christmas broadcast, delivered in a voice that had grown weaker during the past twelve months once more reached out into the hearts of his people. He spoke of their joys and sorrows, and his own; there was a special word for the children and a last patriarchal blessing. The ordeal over, his ebbing strength confined him to the simplest of pleasures. 'Saw my Kent grandson in his bath,' he noted with satisfaction. He rode his fat little shooting pony about the [Sandringham] estate, planted a cedar tree in front of the house, watched his wife arrange Queen Alexandra's collection of Fabergé which had returned to Sandringham after the death of Princess Victoria. But he had not lost his concern for the welfare of others. Having lent the Royal Pavilion, Aldershot, to the recently married Gloucesters as their first home, he took the trouble to write to his daughter-in-law, hoping that she was finding it warm enough.

Alarmed by reports from Sister Black [the King's nurse] of the King's breathlessness, [Lord] Dawson [the Royal doctor] invited himself over to Sandringham from Cambridge on 12 January. 'Found him feeling unwell,' he noted, 'no energy – felt life on top of him – and in conversation said so.'[1]

Over the following days, the King continued to weaken, spending most of the day dozing in front of a fire, and then drifting in and out of consciousness. Sister Agnes wrote a letter of concern and sympathy to her old friend Queen Mary. The Archbishop of Canterbury arrived at Sandringham; and the Prince of Wales left his father for London to consult with the Prime Minister about arrangements for the succession.

Monday, 20th January 1936 was the last day of the King's life. That morning the Archbishop said some simple prayers with him, laid his hands on his Sovereign's head and blessed him. Then, in a lucid moment, the King sent for his Private Secretary. Wigram found him with *The Times* open at the imperial and foreign page. It was some paragraph which had caught his eye, Wigram thought, that prompted the celebrated enquiry, 'How is the Empire?'[2]

The King was never to learn that Dawson arranged the time of his death so that the announcement would be made in the respectable morning newspapers rather than in the disreputable evening papers. This was accomplished by the injection into George V's jugular vein of a deadly dose of morphia and cocaine. The only person to be a witness to this dubious act was Sister Black, who was deeply shocked. The King died shortly before midnight, the last minutes after the injection being tranquil instead of restless as the previous hours had been.

The new King, Edward VIII, was a highly popular figure in the country, much more of a throwback to the extrovert Edward VII than his father. There was a multitude of arrangements to be made, and it was not until 1 April 1936 that Sister Agnes could be reassured that the new King would follow his predecessors and agree to be Patron of her Hospital.

> Privy Purse Office
> Buckingham Palace S.W.

Dear Sister Agnes,

The King wishes to thank you for your letter of March 31st, and to say that he will certainly give his patronage to the hospital. I must ask you however, to say nothing about this for the present, for this reason:

The question of his Majesty's Patronage for London Hospitals is a very difficult one, and the whole matter has been put in Lord Dawson's hands for his advice. It will be some time before we will be able to give a definite answer to all the London hospitals which have applied for a continuance of Royal Patronage, so please treat this as private until you get an official communication.

Yours sincerely,
Alexander Hardinge

By 21 May, however, Lord Wigram, Keeper of the Privy Purse, was able to give formal confirmation.

Next, a new President was required, and Sister Agnes dispatched this characteristic letter to Prince Henry, Duke of Gloucester:

June 6th 1936

Dear Prince Henry,

You can do something very kind for my hospital & for me. The King has become our Patron, and we *all* want *you* to be our President. We all feel we would rather have you than anyone else, & we shall be so glad if you accept. I don't think we shall give you any trouble. The hospital is very flourishing, & was started nearly 36 [actually 36½] years ago. Please look at enclosed. You will see that we have some very good friends on our Council. Sir Philip Chetwode is going to help us, too. Our Council meets on 23rd of June. Unless for an emergency it only meets once a year. We hope to have your answer before that date.

> With my love to the dear
> little Duchess
> I am always Sir
> your very sincere old friend
> Sister Agnes

The Duke replied promptly from the Royal Pavilion, Aldershot:

Dear Sister Agnes,

Many thanks for your letter & kind invitation to become your President which is a great honour for me to accept.

I hope it will continue to go on flourishing under a new President as it has done in the past.

It is such a pity that our rhododendrons are very nearly all over now.

> Yours sincerely,
> Henry

CHAPTER 7

Sister Agnes Grows Old

THE PATRONAGE OF King Edward VIII lasted for only a few months; while his younger brother's lasted until 1952, the year of his death. By the end of 1936 the nation and the Royal Family had endured and survived the abdication crisis, King George VI was on the throne, and Sister Agnes was an old woman of eighty-four. She had slowed down a little, unsurprisingly, but her patients remembered her at this time much as her patients of the Great War had remembered her: brisk, bright and forever on the move except when she was sitting, bolt upright, at her desk in the office at the bottom of the stairs, door open in order that she could check on the comings and goings.

Outside Belgravia the economic crises and unemployment of the 1920s had rapidly given way to international crises and rearmament, which perversely helped reduce the unemployment. The Fascist regimes of Germany, Italy and Japan were leading the world as relentlessly towards war as had Kaiser Wilhelm and Germany and Austro–Hungary before 1914. As if people needed reminding of the threat of war, air-raid shelters were built within sight of the Hospital and in Hyde Park near by anti-aircraft guns pointed their fingers of defiance towards the sky.

Sister Agnes braced herself for war for the third time since she had set up her Hospital. She was not afraid for herself but like every citizen recognized that this next war would involve civilians as well as the armed services.

The letters surviving from or recalling this time depict as well as anything life at 17 Grosvenor Crescent between the world wars, and of Sister Agnes herself. One resident medical officer recalls

two happy years pampered by Butler Wright, ex-Coldstream Guards, complete with a tie pin (Regimental) given to him by King Edward VII, John an excellent valet, a chauffeur who put my car outside every morning and garaged it unless otherwise instructed every evening. All the inmates, including the doctor, had two fingers of whisky after dinner – an excellent idea to ward off the withdrawal symptoms . . .

Another story originating in the 1930s came from a contributor, and was about his father, A. M. Mollison CBE FRCS, who trained at Guy's and became a distinguished ear, nose and throat surgeon:

He started to operate at Sister Agnes's when she was in Grosvenor Crescent. She was not trained and my father was highly amused to find the following note from her when he arrived in the morning to operate:

Dear Mr Mollison,
I am unable to be present at your operation this morning, but have every confidence in leaving the patient in your care.

One Captain RN also recounted how Sister Agnes would some-times take the 'walking wounded' across Grosvenor Place, the traffic grinding to a halt as if she were royalty, and then unlock the little door into Buckingham Palace gardens, and lead in her 'boys'. The King would sometimes join them on the lawn for a chat. Nothing could more comprehensively have completed the patients' recovery.

Major P. B. Hall writes:

I was a Sandhurst cadet in 1938, and attended the nursing home to have an operation for recurrent dislocation of my shoulder. If it was not successful I would not have been commissioned.

I was admitted at the front door by a very tall ex-Coldstreamer who told me that his regiment was second to none. I was later received by Sister

Agnes, who was then aged 86, in a most friendly way. She was very small and slim and wore what appeared to be a blonde wig. At all times she was dressed in immaculate nurse's uniform and visited the wards daily, walking with a stick. She also attended every operation and as I came to from mine I heard her say that it was a beautiful operation. It was carried out by a famous surgeon of the day called Rowley Bristow, who later in the war was promoted Brigadier as Consultant Surgeon to the Army.

Sister Agnes talked about King Edward VII and showed me a gold cup he had given her when his horse Mirabu won the Derby. She had a nice garden behind the nursing home, which she was very keen on . . . The patients were serving and retired officers of all ages ranging from my 20 years to a Colonel of 90 who had come in to have his legs bent straight.

A number of elderly retired officers recall, second to their experiences as patients, the resolution with which they were pursued for subscriptions by their commanding officers. One Royal Engineers officer remembered

our introduction to 'Sister Agnes's' at our first lecture by a pretty forceful adjutant at the School of Military Engineering at Chatham. Amongst the 'compulsory-voluntary' subscriptions which we were 'expected' to make, Sister Agnes's was high on the list – second only, I should think, to the R.E. Widows' Fund. To sweeten the pill, he recommended heartily that, to ensure we got full benefit from our Sister Agnes sub., we should have her name tattoo'd on some outstanding portion of our anatomy . . . In those days we all subscribed 10/- a year – rather more than a day's pay.

The ferocity with which Sister Agnes maintained discipline has been attested to by all who felt the lash of her tongue, be they knighted generals or young subalterns, distinguished surgeons or new young doctors. A major-general, looking back forty-six years, recalled how a group of subalterns from Aldershot delivered one of their number, with a broken neck, strapped to a stretcher and lashed to an open Lagonda car. 'We were received by Sister Agnes herself and got a tremendous rocket, followed by tea!'

Another 'rocket' was noted by a retired brigadier, who was admitted after a skiing accident and shared a ward with five other officers:

Sister Agnes was a very charming old lady but a bit of a martinet. I well remember one morning when she was doing her early morning rounds, she came into our ward, stopped, sniffed and said, 'Who has been smoking before breakfast?' The culprit collected quite a rocket!

This same officer claimed that the only time patients were 'safe' from her eagle eye (and nose) was Sunday before lunch as she had a standing invitation to take a glass of sherry at the Palace.

More seriously, when a young lieutenant twice flouted the smoking regulations (smoking was limited to certain hours) he was told that there would be an ambulance at the door in five minutes. And so there was, with instructions to take him to the enormous St George's Hospital round the corner, where he was found a bed in a public ward.

Captain S. R. Lombard-Hobson CVO OBE RN had an amusing tale to tell of Sister Agnes:

While I was serving as a wee midshipman in the battleship *Queen Elizabeth* (1931) I had a difference of opinion with the PMO who said I had appendicitis. My father, who was some sort of a courtier at the time, rang the Second Sea Lord, Sir Michael Hodges, and between them I was whipped out of the ship and operated on in King Edward VII.

As I was going under, I remember a tiny little lady was holding my hand (she looked a hundred). As I came to back in bed, the same little lady was still holding my hand. I asked her what she was doing, and she said that no patient of hers had ever been on the operating table or afterwards, without her personally checking his pulse rate.

Sister Agnes then said to me, with a most charming smile, 'Young man, you're a fraud, you never had appendicitis.' She then produced out of a spitoon something that looked like a piece of chewing gum. 'As soon as the stitches are out,' she said, 'go straight back to your ship and give this perfectly healthy tissue to your PMO with my compliments!'

The late Lord Adeane, an equerry to the present Queen, recalled:

Sister Agnes used to come to stay with my grandfather every year in Scotland in the hope of being invited to Balmoral, which she usually was.

She was always very kind and used to tip me 10/-, a lot in those days. She was an indomitable character . . . My aunt worked in her Hospital all through the First World War, and she always said that though a strict disciplinarian, Sister Agnes stuck up for the nurses, and could be extremely rough with the doctors, to say nothing of the patients. She admired her very much.

Sister Agnes recognized from the beginning how important the nurses were to the smooth and successful running of her Hospital. She chose them with the utmost care, and attracted their loyalty from the first day. She did not pay them over the odds but looked after them as if they were her own children. One patient commented that 'Sister Agnes sometimes seemed to care more for the nurses than the patients, and that's saying a lot'. In fact every patient was visited at least twice a day, and in critical cases many times day and night.

The nurses tended to be small like herself, well spoken but not necessarily high class. Also like herself, they were perfectly turned out. She addressed them formally – Miss Smith, or sometimes but not often (they were mostly unmarried), Mrs Smith. If they lived in, their accommodation was more than adequate, often sharing with one or two others. These rooms at the top of the house had once been the servants' quarters, but were kept immaculately decorated and as clean as the nurses' uniforms.

The nurses had a lot to put up with, not from Sister Agnes whom they loved, but from boisterous young men on the mend. Captain Aubrey Brooke Winch of the Royal Scots Greys tells of another officer guilty of breaching the smoking rules among other things:

Sister Agnes appeared. She told him that he was not a gentleman and that had he been less ill she would have summoned a taxi to take him away immediately. The sinner was almost under the bedclothes by this time! All the same he was not truly contrite because I remember that same man telling the pretty little nurse that his mother always kissed him last thing at night and it would help him greatly to get to sleep if she did so too!

A retired brigadier, H. E. Cubitt-Smith, offers us a glimpse of life at King Edward VII's in the spring of 1934:

In those days the hospital resembled a comfortable Officer's Mess, with a butler in attendance and with Sister Agnes as Commandant. She was a great little lady, a *law unto herself*. I was to undergo a knee-cap operation. There were three other officers in my upstairs ward – it was the point-to-point and skiing season!

I had recently come home from India, on leave, and on board ship shared a lunch table with Eric Shipton, the mountaineer, Bill Bunie and Norman Phillimore of the 9th Lancers, attached to the Somaliland Camel Corps. Our daily lunch was confined to brandy. We were, after all, *relaxing*!

Judge my surprise at 6 p.m. on my first evening, when the butler arrived and, approaching my bed, displayed a liquor glass of brandy and gravely announced, 'With Mr Phillimore's compliments, sir.' I did not even know that he was an inmate.

My knee was in splints and heavily bandaged after my operation. The same evening the sister in charge informed me that I was to be given morphia. I protested, saying that I was not in pain. I was told it was Sister Agnes's personal instruction. I still refused. In desperation the ward sister asked me if I would lie to Sister Agnes on her evening round. Sure enough the great lady duly enquired if I had been given morphia, and I lied like a trooper. Later I discovered it was one of Sister Agnes's pet fads to prescribe morphia.

The day following I complained to the ward sister that my bandage was too tight. But she was too frightened to take action, saying that Mr Elmslie [the Bart's orthopaedic consultant] had himself tied the bandages. I, therefore, reported my complaint to Sister Agnes. Believe it or not, within a matter of 2 to 3 hours, Mr Elmslie duly appeared. He had been *summoned* by Sister Agnes!

Great man that he was, he admitted that the bandage was too tight.

CHAPTER 8

Sister Agnes's Decline in Her Third War

I N 1939, SISTER Agnes could recall how the Great War had broken
out like a clap of thunder, and wounded officers were at her door
as rapidly as they could be shipped back across the Channel and into
hospital trains at the ports. This time the build-up to a great war was
more measured, and so many crises and so much fighting had already
broken out – in China, Spain, Abyssinia, Albania – that, like beaten
flesh, we had become immune to the agony of dread expectation.

In May 1937, the weary Prime Minister, Stanley Baldwin, resigned,
to be replaced by that arch-exponent of appeasement, Neville
Chamberlain. More parochially, in Belgravia and the rest of London,
the buses disappeared from the streets for two weeks on strike. Sister
Agnes did not use public transport, but it was strange not to see the
big double-deckers swinging round Hyde Park Corner.

In June of that same year, the dashing but abdicated King Edward
VIII, now retitled the Duke of Windsor, married his mistress Wallis
Simpson in France. Sister Agnes had never trusted him and was glad
to have the steadier George VI on the throne and as her Patron, sup-
ported by his reliable wife from Scotland* and two daughters, Princess
Elizabeth and Princess Margaret Rose.

---

* As this was being written the Queen Mother had just emerged from King Edward
VII's after a successful hip-replacement operation – at the age of ninety-five. Later she
had an emergency replacement operation on her other hip.

In October of 1937 ominous riots occurred among the German Sudetens of Czecho–Slovakia, and Italy withdrew from the League of Nations.

The appeasement of the Fascist powers of Germany and Italy continued in 1938; Anthony Eden, the popular British Foreign Secretary, resigned in protest. Lord Halifax replaced him; while in Germany Adolf Hitler appointed himself War Minister.

In spite of all indications to the contrary, few people feared that the horrors of 1914 were going to be repeated. Harold Nicolson, diplomatist and Member of Parliament with close connections to the seats of power, wrote hopefully to his wife in February, 'I do not think there is going to be a war yet. Not by a long chance. And if we can gain two years of peace, then we are almost out of the wood.'[1] But a month later (15 March 1938) his tone had changed radically, and he wrote in his diary, 'A sense of danger and anxiety hangs over us like a pall. Hitler has completely collared Austria; no question of an *Anschluss*, just complete absorption.'[2]

As in 1914, the mobilization of reserves spread all over Europe, for the British Royal Navy on 27 September, while at the same time concessions to Italy and Germany continued apace. Prime Minister Neville Chamberlain, in a last-ditch effort to save the peace, flew to Germany. He came home with what was to become a famous piece of paper which purported to guarantee that Germany had no more territorial ambitions in Europe, and that we could expect 'peace in our time'.

All through the spring and summer of 1939, Hitler and Mussolini showed the world that their word meant nothing. Italy invaded Albania; Germany occupied the rest of Czecho–Slovakia. Britain, at last thoroughly alarmed, introduced peacetime conscription for the first time; and Parliament passed through an emergency powers bill.

On 28 August Nicolson wrote in his diary:

It looks as if war will burst upon us tomorrow. Again that curious contrast with 3rd August 1914! Then we were excited by all these events and there was a sense of exhilaration. Today we are merely glum. It is not merely my age and experience which silence me under this leaden cope of gloom.[3]

War did not come until 3 September, after Hitler had invaded Poland. As if to demonstrate his total lack of scruples, he ordered the bombing of open towns and Warsaw itself.

Sister Agnes had her last peacetime Council meeting on 11 July 1939 as the crisis was racing to a head. The Secretary read out to the meeting the Patron's usual message:

> I have received the following message from the King who, as Patron of King Edward VII's Hospital for Officers, takes a personal interest in its prosperity and progress.
>
> His Majesty is glad to know that after thirty-nine years the Hospital continues to flourish, and desires to express to all who work for it his sincere congratulations and good wishes.

The imminent threat of war was the most important item on the agenda. Harold Wernher, Chairman, was in an authoritative position having earlier in the year served on a government committee which was making plans for dealing with civilian casualties if and when war broke out again. The figures estimated by the Air Ministry were 'terrifying', according to Wernher. The chairman of that committee was Sir Charles Wilson, later Lord Moran, who became Churchill's doctor, and Churchill himself wrote, 'I knew that the Government were prepared, in the first few days of the war, with over 250,000 beds for air-raid casualties.'[4]

Now, at Grosvenor Crescent, the Council decided unanimously to move the Hospital out of London if war came. Before this meeting Harold had spoken to his mother, now Lady Ludlow, who had lived at Luton Hoo since Julius's death, and had raised the question of a home for the Hospital in the event of evacuation. She had at once suggested her own house, which was big enough to accommodate a dozen Grosvenor Crescent houses, so the disruption would be very slight.

The offer was now accepted gratefully by the Council, and when war was declared less than two months later, the machinery to carry out the move was already turning over as the sounds of the first air-raid warning were heard in Belgravia. (A false alarm as it turned out.)

A few days later, Sister Agnes was writing to Clive Wigram, lord-in-waiting and extra equerry to George VI:

> c/o Lady Ludlow
> Luton Hoo
> *September 10 1939*

Clive dear,

I [would] like you to know that I have moved the whole hospital here. It is a heavenly place & will make a beautiful hospital.

It was a terrible move & we just got here in time. I feel very far away from you all but I know you will think of me.

It is my third war.

Always your affectionate
Sister Agnes[5]

This move put a great strain on Sister Agnes, who was now eighty-seven, but she was determined to hang on as Matron and make a success of King Edward VII's Hospital in its new location. Alas, this was not to be. One of the chief attractions of 17 Grosvenor Crescent was its intimacy. As many people remarked, it was more like staying in a club than a hospital. It was also convenient for the doctors and surgeons as well as for the recruitment of nursing staff. Luton Hoo, for all its grandeur, lacked these advantages. The patients did not come.

After one of the coldest winters on record, the Council made the decision that the Hospital should return to Grosvenor Crescent. This was as great a mistake as the move to Luton Hoo, but there were no precedents for this situation: a great capital city at war without fighting, and the massive machinery available to deal with catastrophe remaining unused. Even after the evacuation of Dunkirk, only a handful of wounded officers sought out Sister Agnes. One of these was 2nd Lieutenant Douglas Bright of the Oxfordshire and Buckingham Light Infantry, whose father had been a patient in about 1906. He writes today as a retired brigadier:

In May 1940 I was wounded on the French–Belgian border and was evacuated to an emergency hospital in Hertfordshire. My mother came to see me and realized that I was not in a very good state. She wrote to Sister

Agnes, mentioning the link with my father, and asking her to agree to take me in. The next thing that happened was that an ambulance, with a doctor, arrived to collect me to Sister Agnes's. I was discharged from there the following August.

Sister Agnes toured the wards every morning, wearing a scarlet wig, an unauthorized uniform, and the Royal Red Cross. She knew all the patients, and the nurses discouraged you from smoking until after her visit! When you were convalescent, you had lunch with her in the dining-room and she carved the joint personally. The care and medical attention of the Hospital was, of course, of the highest standard.

There were still only one or two officer patients when the Battle of Britain began on 10 July. Bombs occasionally fell on London during July and August, and on one frantic and memorable day a German bomber came down low and flew up the Mall from Trafalgar Square, aiming for Buckingham Palace. Sister Agnes saw none of this but heard the explosion of the bombs, which hit their target, above the sound of the guns.

Then on 7 September the first heavy night raid on London took place. Great fires broke out at the Surrey Docks and elsewhere. It seemed as if the whole city was ablaze. Nearly five hundred civilians died in this holocaust, and many more were seriously injured. It was a precursor of what was to come when thousands would die in a single night of bombing.

Harold Wernher telephoned Sister Agnes the following day, and between them they decided to close down 17 Grosvenor Crescent again for the time being. Within a week the house was empty of patients and staff, who were distributed among London's big teaching hospitals. It was an agonizing step to take, especially as she feared it would be thought that she had capitulated in the face of the enemy. In fact she was not in the least frightened or provoked by the bombing, and had by no means despaired of opening up King Edward VII's elsewhere.

For the present, however, she packed a trunk or two with her clothes and a few of her smaller precious possessions and took the train to Faringdon in the West Country, where she had a standing invitation to stay with her old friend, Lady Fitzgerald, Amelia, one of the

Bischoffsheim family, who had married Sir Maurice Fitzgerald, 20th Knight of Kerry. He had died in 1927.

The reason for the first mighty night attack on London was the assumption of power by Hermann Goering of the air battle against Britain. It was he, and he alone, who had made the decision to switch the main attack to London itself. In tactical terms this was a great folly. Many of the airfields from which Fighter Command was operating had been made inoperable or had been so badly damaged that a few more days of daylight attack could have wiped them out. This respite gave Fighter Command time to repair the airfields and communications and build up its complement of fighter aircraft.

Goering wanted to make London uninhabitable and to destroy its industrial buildings and docks, and thereby halt their activities. For this reason the early night bombing was concentrated on the east of the city. Belgravia for the present received only a scattering of bombs. Nevertheless, morale throughout the city was low, as described by Winston Churchill:

> From September 7 to November 3 an average of two hundred German bombers attacked London every night. The various preliminary raids which had been made upon our provincial cities in the previous three weeks had led to a considerable dispersion of our anti-aircraft artillery, and when London first became the main target there were but ninety-two guns in position. It was thought better to leave the air free for our night-fighters . . . Of these there were six squadrons of Blenheims and Defiants. Night-fighting was in its infancy, and very few casualties were inflicted on the enemy. Our batteries therefore remained silent for three nights in succession. Their own technique was at this time woefully imperfect. Nevertheless, in view of the weakness of our night-fighters and of their unsolved problems it was decided that the anti-aircraft gunners should be given a free hand to fire at unseen targets, using any methods of control they liked.
>
> For three nights Londoners had sat in their houses or inadequate shelters enduring what seemed to be an utterly unresisted attack. Suddenly, on September 10, the whole barrage opened, accompanied by a blaze of

searchlights. This roaring cannonade did not do much harm to the enemy, but gave enormous satisfaction to the population. Everyone was cheered by the feeling that we were hitting back . . .[6]

Down in Faringdon, Sister Agnes did not find that all was peace and quiet. The sky was full of aeroplanes, but at least they were not lethal; they were training machines, quiet Airspeed Oxfords and Tiger Moths, and noisier Harvards. Berkshire, Gloucestershire and Oxfordshire were spotted with training airfields, and the sound of aeroplane engines was continuous day and night.

During those autumn days of 1940, the cessation of her work and responsibility had a profound effect on Sister Agnes. The breaks in her working life since 1899 had been brief, and despite the odd long weekend at Balmoral, Sandringham or one of the many country houses where she was always welcome, she had never felt any loss of control over her Hospital, the running of which had become her life.

Here at Buckland House, however, for all the kindness and consideration of her friend, she felt the machinery of her life had wound down, and she was too old and tired to rewind it. In order to keep in touch, she wrote to her friends and she read the newspapers, which were full of reports on the bombing of London and other cities, like Coventry where six hundred tons of high-explosive bombs and thousands of incendiaries smashed the heart out of the city on one November night.

Sister Agnes and Lady Fitzgerald continued with their crossword puzzles and with taking turns about the gardens, while raids on the capital reached new heights. On 29 December 1940, an incendiary raid on the City of London did untold damage: eight Wren churches were destroyed and the damage to docks and railway stations was terrible, while fifteen hundred fires had to be fought. This author bears witness to the fact that the glow from the flames was visible more than twenty miles away.

The bombing of London continued into the New Year. On 12 January Sir George Ogilvie, Sister Agnes's last House Governor, telephoned her to say that 16 and 17 Grosvenor Crescent had just received a direct hit and were in ruins. He was sorry to give her this bad news, but felt she ought to know. She took the news calmly and asked him if he could pick her up in his car and drive her to London. He was with her very quickly, for there was almost no traffic. Once in the heart of London Sister Agnes saw plenty of evidence of the four months of bombing since she had last been in the city. There were frequent gaps in the terraces of shops and houses, which looked like jaws from which teeth had been forcibly extracted. A number of streets were shut off entirely, with steel-helmeted police or air-raid wardens on guard beside the protective ropes. There were piles of uncleared rubble, glinting with broken glass, and suffocating masonry dust filled the air.

The smart houses in Park Lane had not been immune and Sister Agnes noted the absence of some of her friends' homes. By the time the car had reached Hyde Park Corner, she was feeling sick from the shock, and the fervour with which men were digging at the rubble of some houses, suggesting survivors, added to her distress. Sir George's chauffeur turned right into Grosvenor Crescent, and she told him to slow down. The rubble from her home was spilled half-way across the road, confirming how recent was the damage, and the absence of anyone working on the skeletal remains suggested that it was known that the two houses had been uninhabited. She got out, a tiny, frail figure amongst all this evidence of the brutality of war, leaning heavily on the stick that had supported her for so many years about the wards and corridors of her Hospital. Some neighbours, recognizing her, came out into the street and waited tentatively for her to return and speak to them. All she said, with great firmness, was, 'We must find another house in Belgravia when this is over.' Then she got back into the car and was driven away.

Sister Agnes was never to see the report on the incident although this later became available to Harold Wernher and others of the Hospital Council.

The bomb, certainly an H.E. [high explosive] and probably of 250 kg had fallen at precisely 8 o'clock on the evening of 11 January. It struck the rear of the Victoria Club, 9 Halkin Street and the rear of 16 and 17 Grosvenor Crescent, demolishing all three buildings. Nine people were killed at the Victoria Club, and the two caretakers at no. 17 were also casualties. No one was trapped in the rubble, and a stretcher party and ambulance, despatched at 8.19 p.m., were soon on the scene. There were four more ambulance cases from nearby buildings lacking shelters, and the Post [air-raid] Warden treated several people caught out in the street and slightly injured, probably by flying glass.[7]

Sister Agnes had been in frail health for some time. To keep up her morale and the optimism which had ruled all her life, she had been looking for a house in the Home Counties in which she could resume her life's work, and had even visited one or two. But Lady Fitzgerald must have noticed that after her London visit her friend had lost her spirit. She had not been physically well for some time and, unsurprisingly at her age – she was eighty-eight – became easily tired and spent more time in bed. The coming of spring in no way raised her morale.

Sister Agnes was not forgotten either by her friends or by her old nursing staff. The King and Queen were concerned about her condition, and on 14 April 1941, King George VI sent her a telegram:

The Queen and I are so sorry to hear your Hospital was bombed up in the recent raids & that you yourself are now laid up. We hope that you will soon be fully recovered, so that you can continue your splendid work.

To Buckland House
Faringdon[8]

She also corresponded with her old friend, the widowed Queen Mary, who had been persuaded to leave London for Badminton House; although it was not far from Faringdon, the two old ladies never met at this time. It is apparent from the following letter that the Queen Mother had sent Sister Agnes a present:

Buckland House
Faringdon

To Queen Mary   *Sunday 1941*

My dearest,
    Nothing could give me half the pleasure that the book *from you has given me* . . . I haven't yet got over the shock of the destruction of the two houses

and the loss of my treasures. Lady Fitzgerald & I lead very quiet lives by ourselves, & we never see anybody.

Good bye my dear friend.

Always your very affectionate

Sister Agnes

[In Queen Mary's writing:]

Last letter from dear old Sister Agnes to me a few weeks before she died in May 1941.[9]

The local doctor called frequently and gave Sister Agnes tonics and encouragement, but in the second week of May 1941, she took to her bed. She never arose from it. She awoke seldom and, in the presence of only Lady Fitzgerald and her doctor, faded away on Sunday 11 May, just four months after her Hospital had been destroyed.

The world was told of her death with this last message in the deaths column of *The Times*:

KEYSER On May 11, 1941, at Buckland House, Faringdon, Agnes Keyser. 'Sister Agnes', 'This is just to say good-bye to my dear patients and friends all over the world.' Funeral at Great Stanmore: date to be announced later.

Six days later *The Times* carried a formal account of the funeral, Queen Mary being represented by Major the Hon. John Coke, and officiating were the Bishop of Shrewsbury, the Rev. R. S. Swann-Mason, Chaplain to the Hospital, and the Rev. W. A. Hewett. Among the Keysers present were Mr and Mrs Norman Keyser, Miss Muriel Keyser, and Miss Sybil Keyser. Sir Rowland and Lady Sperling were among other close relatives. It was a packed congregation including titled representatives of the armed services. Also present was Sister Thomas, who represented the nurses of Sister Agnes's Hospital; they were all employed elsewhere and now, with their founder dead, never expected it to reopen. Lord Dawson of Penn, the King's doctor and the most distinguished figure in medicine at that time, wrote to Sir George Ogilvie on 14 May 1941:

Dear Sir George,

Your wire brought me relief. Personality and death of the body do not coincide in their passing and I dreaded her lingering on when the real Sister Agnes has left us.

I thought her message of farewell was charming.

Thank you for letting me know.

Yours sincerely,

Dawson

The Times noted in its obituary that the news of Sister Agnes's death would be received 'with particular sorrow in the services'. A condensed history of the origins and progress of the Hospital followed:

From 1900 to 1930 nearly 11,000 officers were treated, mostly surgical cases. Sister Agnes having assisted at practically all the operations. In 1926, her sister, known by many in the Services as Miss Fanny, died. Sister Agnes never really recovered from this loss, but, in spite of ill health, she attended daily to the work of the Hospital.

As a young woman, Miss Keyser was strikingly beautiful, with her fair hair, blue eyes, and exquisite colouring, and she retained her charm of manner as the years passed. Her Hospital had been for forty years the sole interest and care of her life, and to it she devoted all her gifts of organization and management . . .

It may now be added that both King Edward and King George wished to recognize Sister Agnes's work by the conferment to some high honour, but on each occasion she asked permission to decline.

An additional 'Appreciation' appeared in *The Times* two days later, 15 May 1941:

It would seem almost impossible for officers of the Army to pay adequate tribute to Sister Agnes . . . All who were privileged to be her patients will record a debt of deep gratitude to a great benefactress and affectionate memories of her kindness and hospitality.

As one who, as a junior subaltern before the last war, and again 15 years later, was a patient under her care, one has vivid recollections of her wonderful personality. Her entry into the room when one was ill or depressed, her kindliness, her attention to the smallest detail in the administration and welfare of her patients, and, perhaps above all, her cheerfulness at all times, were the best possible medicine for the sick and sorry. Her kind, tactful, yet firm discipline, both with patients and staff, were an outstanding characteristic of her administration. Yet this added to one's respect without diminishing one's affection . . .

It adds to, rather than detracts from, the picture of Sister Agnes that she had her eccentricities and even rather cranky ways. For example, except for her nurses, she did not much like to have women, even wives of patients, about her Hospital. If she thought that women visitors had overstayed their time, she chivvied them away. One brigadier recalled his mother telling him about his father's experiences: 'She liked to keep in touch with her ex-patients, & see them socially from time to time, but *only* as long as they remained bachelors! Once they married all interest and contact ended.'

Married officers were no longer 'my boys', and she did not care for her influence to be diluted.

Sister Agnes's protectiveness towards her patients was matched by her refusal to give up hope. In October 1915 a captain in the Royal Welsh Fusiliers, who had heard of her magic touch, made his own way to Grosvenor Gardens and asked to be admitted. He had a rifle bullet in his right shoulder and numerous shrapnel wounds. His son, Major Nigel Kearsley, writes that 'at the base hospital he overheard the medical officer saying to the Matron, "We'll have to take his arm off tomorrow." He duly escaped from the hospital that night and found his way across the Channel to Dover.'

Mr Sherren took the young man in hand, and Kearsley underwent a series of operations to his right shoulder and thigh. He remained under Sister Agnes's care for thirteen months. 'Under her personal supervision,' continues the son, 'his arm was mended and, although it was always weak, he became a leading horseman between the wars and died aged 93 in 1976. He was eternally grateful to Sister Agnes for this.'

The lighter side of Sister Agnes is remembered by many patients.

Major-General Roger St John CB MC has a droll tale to recount about his father, Major B. T. St John of the 5th Fusiliers:

[My father was] evacuated from Boulogne in 1915 to Sister Agnes's with his windpipe ruptured by a bullet amongst other wounds and in a poor condition.

Here he came under the eminent Dr Harmer and underwent a considerable number of operations, mostly without anaesthetic. He was there for two years or so and of course was devoted to Sister Agnes. She invariably sat with him for his operations holding his hand and offering comforting and cheerful chat.

Towards the end of his time there, recovering and now tubed like a horse, he got fed up, along with others, with the bossiness of a particular middle-aged VAD battleaxe. In order to enliven her day he made his way to his daily bath with only a bowler hat, umbrella and sock suspenders on and made a point of meeting her head on! She made a fearful fuss and reported him to Sister Agnes who roared with laughter and removed the battleaxe from further duties!

Commander Robert Hennessy LVO DSC recalls two drink-related incidents in 1937:

I well remember Sister Agnes with her bright red wig and stick doing the evening rounds. I was just recovering from the anaesthetic on the first occasion and she said, 'Give the boy some champagne to liven him up.' I was a sub-lieutenant at the time. On the day of the Grand National, 1937, we were given some very good vintage port after dinner, a present from the Duke of Gloucester.

By contrast with the lighter side of Sister Agnes are tales of the terror she inspired in patients and surgeons alike. Michael Ramsay MBE writes:

My father was a surgeon, and frequently operated at the Hospital in the '20s and '30s. One day he was told that Sister Agnes wished to see him. Not knowing what was in store, he duly appeared before her. Without looking up from her desk, she said, 'No, no, this will not do *at all* . . .' My father shook in his shoes. After a while she looked up, and finally smiled, and said, 'Oh, it's Mr Ramsay; I had been expecting someone else.' My father never learnt who was the unfortunate victim of her displeasure.

Perhaps the best of all renderings of Sister Agnes is provided by the recollections of a child's eyes' view, in this case by a great-nephew, who became Brigadier E. G. B. Davies-Scoursfield:

To us children (my brothers, sisters and me) Aunt Aggie was an awesome figure: perhaps we never knew her well enough to perceive the twinkle in her eye and her tremendous sense of fun. Indeed the prospect of being taken to lunch with her was a little nerve-racking. For several days before such an august occasion my mother used to make us practise sitting at meals bolt upright on the forward edge of our chairs, for such would Aunt Aggie expect: it was exactly how she always sat herself. I do not remember Aunt Fanny who must have died when I was very young.

My mother used to take us separately to lunch with Aunt Aggie. We used to arrive very punctually on these occasions even though we were usually kept waiting for a considerable time: Aunt Aggie was invariably detained in the operating theatre of her Hospital. We understood that she attended all the operations. While we waited we would admire her huge collection of signed photographs of members of the Royal Family, all beautifully framed and spread around her drawing-room. She was immensely proud of these photographs and of her friendships with such important people.

'You know,' she once told me, 'I have my own special key into the garden of Buckingham Palace, so that I can so conveniently exercise my dog.'

We children, as we grew a little older, used to speculate on the precise nature of her great friendship with Edward VII, and if we wanted to tease my mother we would suggest to her that perhaps the friendship could possibly have been a little more than merely platonic. My mother would rise to the bait and retort fiercely that 'Aunt Aggie was not that sort of person at all'.

One officer, who was a patient in her Hospital, remembers her, coming on her rounds, saying to him, 'This room was once my bedroom: it's lucky walls have neither ears nor tongues.'

During the First World War my Uncle Noel (Aunt Aggie's nephew) was wounded in France and came to 9 Grosvenor Gardens. Apparently in those days smoking was allowed in the wards but only at certain times. One day she caught him smoking at the wrong moment and warned him, 'Being my nephew does not give you licence to break my rules. If I find you doing so again a hansom cab will be immediately summoned and you will find yourself in St George's within half an hour.'

Although I believe she had neither any medical training nor any qualifications, she ruled her Hospital with a rod of iron and stood no non-sense from anyone. My eldest brother was once her patient for some operation when he was about eighteen years old, carried out by a very eminent surgeon. She told my brother that the bill for this treatment would not be excessive. 'Oh,' said my brother, 'Sir John (or whatever) has told me that he won't be charging me too much.'

'Indeed,' said Aunt Aggie, who immediately strode off to find the unfortunate Sir John and told him that if he ever discussed such concessions with patients again he would never more operate in her Hospital.

On one occasion when my mother took me, aged sixteen, to lunch with her, she asked my mother, 'What is the young man going to do in life?' She did not ask me but addressed her query to my mother, in a rather 'does he take sugar?' manner.

'Well,' replied my mother, 'he wants to go into the Army like his two brothers, but I don't think it's a good idea.'

'And why is it not a good idea?' said Aunt Aggie. 'I cannot think of a finer or more honourable profession than the Army for any young man.'

'Well,' said my mother, 'I feel that at least one of my sons should go into business and try to restore the family fortunes.'

'But he might go into business and lose everything,' said Aunt Aggie. 'Some people do, you know.'

'But I know what will happen,' said my mother. 'All three of them will end up as retired colonels living in Cheltenham.'

'Maybe,' replied Aunt Aggie, 'they won't all three live long enough to be retired colonels. You let the boy do what he wants.' And so she did, and so I owe to that lunchtime conversation something of my extremely happy Army life beginning in 1938 and ending in 1973.

It is hardly surprising therefore that I remember my 'Aunt Aggie' – 'Sister Agnes' to countless officers of several generations – with admiration, gratitude and respect.

Sister Agnes's will was typically long and complex; dated 5 February 1941, and therefore after the bombing of number 17, it suggests that some at least of her private possessions had been removed when she had left London. One clause reads:

> To my dear friend Queen Mary, two tables standing in the window of my dining room at no. 16; To dear Princess Mary the silver elephant cigarette lighter given to me by King Edward; To the Duke of Gloucester the original picture of 'Three of Us' by Miss E. A. Drage; To Florence Lady de la Rue the gold purse given to me by King George and Queen Mary and a little gold cup given to me by King Edward . . .

As to bequests, these varied from £500 to her two butlers and her lady's maid, who also got the whole of her wardrobe, to £50 each to anyone who was still in her employ after more than three years.

Nurses and sisters who had worked for her were all remembered generously, but it was the Hospital itself which was the chief beneficiary, being left all her leasehold properties, a sum of £25,000 and, at the conclusion of the will 'the rest of my estate and effects . . .' Harold Wernher, a nephew Sir Rowland Sperling, and her nieces Muriel and Sybil Keyser were executors and trustees.

PART 2

Marylebone

CHAPTER 9

Rebirth

I T IS A measure of Sister Agnes's single-minded powers of organization and enduring dedication that no other individual or body
attempted during the Second World War to found a similar hospital catering for the needs which she had provided throughout the
First World War.

If she had been ten years younger she no doubt would have been
fired to reopen in spite of the bombings: plenty of other hospitals and
nursing homes in London remained open. In 1939 there was a powerful Council, including Lieutenant-Colonel Sir George Ogilvie,
who had had a distinguished career in the Indian Government, and
Sir Philip Chetwode, a Field Marshal, and later a peer.

The one man who kept a thread of life going from the old Hospital
was Ogilvie, who managed the invested funds and was responsible for
assisting subscribers with their nursing or hospital expenses after the
Hospital closed. When the course of war allowed, he also began to
look around for new premises for a post-war revival; in spite of Sister
Agnes's words over the ruins of 16 and 17 Grosvenor Crescent, he did
not look in Belgravia.

Though he was not at that time actively involved, the other figure
whose thoughts, even in the hurly-burly of world war, returned again
and again to the revival of King Edward VII's Hospital, was Harold
Wernher.

*

As for countless other people, the opening days of the war brought with them many problems for the Wernhers. Harold and Zia were in no way protected from these by their wealth. Zia evacuated all the children from the children's home she had earlier set up in Hampstead, to her mother-in-law's gigantic place, Luton Hoo. They were billeted there in the laundry and stable flats.

At Lubenham arrangements were made to dispose of the horses, and the farm was modified to a more realistic basis, the production of food being paramount. For the present, anyway, fox-hunting was over, like so many peacetime pleasures. The 'phoney' war period was frozen in more than one sense. It was a bitterly cold winter and discontent and uncertainty stalked the land. The awakening – the occupation of most of Europe by the German armies, the defeat of France and the retreat to Dunkirk and elsewhere by the British Expeditionary Forces (BEF) – was as bad as the waiting.

Like everyone else, Harold and Zia were forced to come to terms with reality. Harold, over age but filled with energy and anger, used his influence to acquire from the United States a million rifles and automatic weapons for the newly formed Local Defence Volunteers (immortalized many years later in the television series *Dad's Army*.) He eventually was appointed General Staff Officer (GSO1) of South-Eastern Command under Lieutenant-General Bernard Montgomery, and travelled widely in the Home Counties inspecting units. Zia, meanwhile, held equal responsibilities in the St John Ambulance Brigade.

> Her capacity for organization came into full play. She was notoriously outspoken, saying exactly what she thought, yet she could be tactful when inspecting private houses that might be used as annexes for hospitals. One lady was embarrassed because her floors were not carpeted. 'Much better,' Zia said kindly. 'It's healthier to have rugs.'[1]

With the Blitz at its height Harold engaged a suite of rooms at the Dorchester Hotel. The word had got about that steel and concrete structures were better able to stand up to high explosive, while the fire risk was also reduced.

Harold needed a base in London in order to conduct his campaign for an appointment to a more important role in the war. It was not until March 1942 that he received the appointment he believed he deserved. Already extensive plans were being made for the invasion and liberation of northern Europe, and Harold was appointed Co-ordinator of Port Facilities, with the rank of Brigadier; his directive from Lord Mountbatten, Chief of Combined Operations, read, 'Your responsibility will embrace the whole problem of preparing facilities for the launching of the Assault and of maintaining supplies and rein-forcements during the earlier phase of a major Combined Operation against Northern France.'

When the directive went into detail it became evident that Harold's task was to be enormous and highly technical, requiring complete control of coastal shipping, railways and roads, measures that would make possible the landing on an open coast not only of tens of thou-sands of men, but their transport, tanks, artillery and supplies of all kinds. 'Mulberry', the unique harbours that went up and down with the tide, and 'Pluto' ('Pipe Line Under the Ocean') for the supply of millions of gallons of oil, both came within Harold's brief.

As the date for the invasion approached, Harold, now promoted to Major-General, became more and more deeply involved, attending the Anglo–American conferences that made the crucial decisions and decided the command structure.

Zia was as busy as Harold, but both were held up in their tracks at the devastating news that their beloved son Alex had died in North Africa where he was fighting with the 17th 21st Lancers. Neither of them fully recovered from this loss.

Harold's commission terminated before the D-Day landings, but he was able to satisfy himself that the immensely elaborate arrange-ments he had co-ordinated worked wonderfully well. He had always feared that the weather could be a greater threat than the German defenders. It was the Supreme Commander, General Dwight D. Eisenhower, who rightly delayed the departure of the landing craft because of the rough weather, and then decided that this greatest combined operation in the history of warfare should go ahead on 6 June 1944. The landings, as the world was told a day later, were a triumphant success, but the weather got its revenge less than two weeks later when an exceptional storm played havoc with the further landing of supplies and totally destroyed one of the two great Mulberry harbours.

The war in Europe ground on for almost another year but at last came to a successful conclusion in May 1945. In December Lady Ludlow died and Harold renewed his hospital work, being elected chairman of University College Hospital, London. He also regained contact with all that remained of King Edward VII's Hospital through the good offices of Sir George Ogilvie, and discovered that the old House Governor had found a bomb-damaged nursing home in Beaumont Street, Marylebone, which might be a good location for the Hospital to re-open. The advantages were its proximity to the heart of medical country – Harley Street, Wimpole Street, Devonshire Street, Welbeck Street and so on – and the fact that the structure of the building, which was largely intact, was of recent (1930) construction in steel and concrete. Harold thoroughly approved and set the wheels in motion for its purchase from the owner, Miss A. Duncanson. Terms were eventually agreed at £45,450, about 75 per cent of which was put up by the War Damage Commission.

Architects were engaged, and by early 1948 work was begun. It was a difficult time for building, both labour and materials being short, but hospital work received priority, and Harold was good at getting things done. A contemporary Hospital statement reads:

Beaumont House was completed and furnished by the Autumn of 1948, and it was formally reopened by Sister Agnes's old friend, Queen Mary, on the 5th October. His Royal Highness the Duke of Gloucester accompanied Her Majesty and there was a large and distinguished gathering to witness the ceremony. A speech was delivered by Major-General Sir Harold Wernher, Chairman of the Hospital, and Her Majesty then declared the Hospital open. She said that the Hospital would be a memorial not only to Sister Agnes but also to her sister Miss Fanny Keyser.

Harold's speech on the same occasion concluded:

There were 22 beds in 17 Grosvenor Crescent, and there are 31 beds in Beaumont House, 16 in wards which will be free and 15 in single rooms

1. The young
Agnes Keyser

2. King
Edward VII

3. Boer War: helping the
wounded at Driefontein
(reconstruction by
photographer after battle)

4. Boer War: field dressing station at Modderrivier

5. Sister Agnes
in evening dress,
c. 1906

6. Sister Agnes
wearing her Red
Cross medal, *c.* 1906

7. No. 17 Grosvenor Crescent, the Keyser sisters' home and first hospital

8. The patients' sitting-room at 9 Grosvenor Gardens

9. The funeral procession of King Edward VII, 20 May 1910,
with the late King's charger and favourite dog Caesar

10. First World War: British trenches on the Somme

11. British wounded at an advance station

12. A British field ambulance, *c.* 1914

13. Stretcher-bearers transporting the wounded from the trenches to a base hospital

14. A First World War Red Cross ambulance car

15. John Lockhart-Mummery, leading surgeon at Sister Agnes's Hospital

admitted
Jan: 17: 15

Mr. Sherren.

left hosp
Jan. 31: 15
to No 17

Diagnosis
bullet wound
of shoulder

Lieut: Matear   Royal Warwick

Oct: 31: 14 wounded near Ypres.
Shrapnel shell wound of left shoulder
entered near clavicle, exit lower part
of Scapula.
Had Staphylococcic infection
now
has large open wound over left Scapula.
healed rapidly.

---

admitted
Oct: 31: 15

Mr. Paterson

left hosp.
Nov: 8: 15.

diagnosis
Shrapnel w
left shoulder.

Lieut: H. O. Dixon 4th The Buffs
30 yrs.   5½ years serv.
wounded Oct: 12: 15 at Suvla Bay
Shrapnel wound of left shoulder
entry at back outside shoulder
passed downwards and
lodged near Elbow.
Oct: 14: 15. Operation
piece of shell removed.
Nov: 8: 15. operation wound healed, entry w. healing
Xray small fragment of metal in arm
to be left in Situ

16. Two pages from Sister Agnes's record book of 1915

17. Sister Agnes visiting Buckingham Palace Gardens, from a newspaper article

18. The German surrender at Field Marshal Montgomery's tactical headquarters, Lüneburg Heath, on 4 May 1945. Photograph of a painting by Terence Cuneo which hangs today in the Hospital

19. This Union flag was flown by Montgomery at his tactical headquarters on the same day. He later presented it to the Hospital

20. Sir Harold
Wernher
(chairman),
Queen Mary,
Matron Alice
Saxby and Sir
George Ogilvie
(house governor)
at the opening of
Beaumont
House, 15
October 1948

21. Queen Mary and Matron Saxby with the nursing staff on the same occasion

22. A photograph of Sister Agnes, taken from *Queen* magazine,
8 November 1950

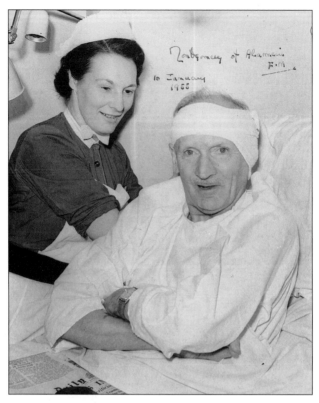

23. Field
Marshal
Montgomery
after his
operation
at the
Hospital in
January 1955

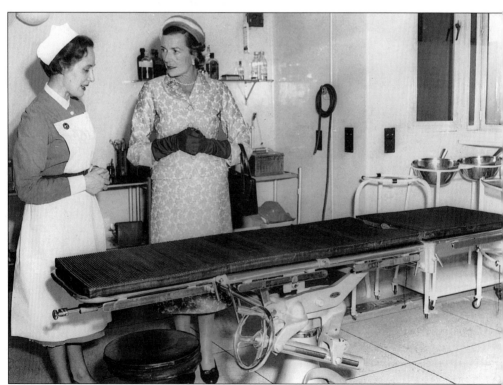

24. Lady Mountbatten in the operating theatre with Sister Ford, 25 September 1956

25. Matron
Saxby, Sir
Harold Wernher
and HM Queen
Elizabeth, the
Queen Mother,
at the opening
of the nurses'
home on 28
November 1957

26. HRH the Duke of Kent and HM Queen Elizabeth, the Queen Mother,
at the opening of the new physiotherapy department in 1980

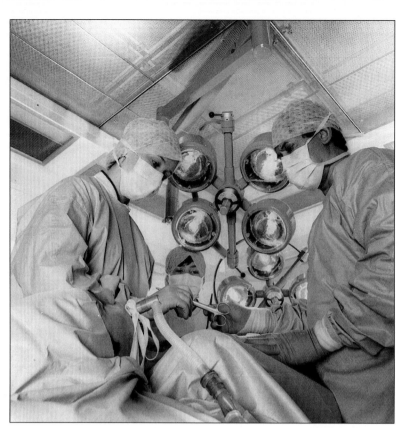

27. One of the Hospital's operating theatres in 1997

28. Nurses, 1997

which will be charged for, though the charge will be less than in other nursing homes of comparable status in London . . . The Hospital has been disclaimed by the Minister of Health under the National Health Service and will in the future require all the good will and support that the Services and general public can give it. It will be open not only to officers of the three Services both serving and retired, but also to all officers who served in the war and who hold emergency and temporary commissions.

One foible Sister Agnes had, if it can be so called, was a profound dislike, almost a horror, of publicity. She even left instructions to her relatives that no formal memorial should be set up after her death. It will be remembered that, although she was ever ready to help ex-patients and friends, she declined all honours for herself. Her wishes were respected, but, whether she would have desired it or not, this new Hospital will be a memorial which the Council hope will keep her memory green for many years to come and will be a permanent tribute to a very great lady and a very great friend.

For members who had served on the Council before the closure in 1940, the contrast between 17 Grosvenor Crescent and Beaumont Street was most marked. At Beaumont House, beautifully decorated and furnished as they were, the wards were undoubtedly wards. There was a dining-room for those patients who could and wished to use it; there was also a very comfortable sitting-room, and even a chapel. But however hard the Council and the architects and decorators tried, Beaumont House would never be anything other than a medical institution. The atmosphere of an exclusive gentleman's club had died with the old Hospital.

Viewing the building from across the busy Marylebone street, no one could confuse Beaumont House with any private dwelling. Handsome it certainly was and has remained to this day, but it was clearly purpose built as a hospital. The same could not be said of the two previous homes of King Edward VII's Hospital – all handsome stucco delicately balanced for domestic use by the original architect of most of Belgravia, Thomas Cubitt.

The two key figures in the running of Beaumont House were the Chairman, Sir Harold Wernher, and the House Governor, Sir George

Ogilvie; the latter was feeling his eighty-four years, and increasingly let it be known. Ogilvie persuaded his daughter, the Hon. Vere Birdwood, to give him a hand. She already had a job which she enjoyed as research secretary of the National Association of Boys Clubs, but agreed to come for six months. In 1950, little more than a year after the reopening, Ogilvie retired, and to her astonishment Vere was asked to take over under the simpler new title of Secretary – in those days you could not style a woman as House Governor. This remarkably efficient woman remained at Beaumont House not for six months but for twenty-two years.

Of her Chairman she once wrote, 'Sir Harold was marvellous, leaving you alone to get on with it. Sometimes he realized you needed backing up. He was a hard man, but fair, and always had an eye for the coming man. He never missed the monthly meetings . . .'

The first problem the Council had to face was the tedious business of fund-raising. Not only was Beaumont House more expensive to run than the old Hospital, but the days were also gone when Sister Agnes could have words with King Edward VII, who in turn would have words with some of his richer cronies, mainly Jewish and mainly in the City, and substantial sums would arrive at the Hospital's bank in Cavendish Square. Things worked differently now.

Besides, Sister Agnes had been a one-woman fund-raiser, as well as dedicated administrator, in her own right. Her network of benefactors was as neat and complex as any spider's web. Her charm was infinite, to the point where her connections regarded contributing as an honour. Harold Wernher recognized that, like Electrolux at Luton, they would have to lay foundations on which to build a structure – and speedily. A House and Finance Committee was formed under the chairmanship of Major R. N. 'Reggie' Macdonald-Buchanan, a member of the Council, as were the other twelve members.

One of the first steps taken to ensure a full flow of patients, and thus income, was to draw up a Supplemental Charter to extend the number of those qualified to apply for a bed:

Early in 1950 a Humble Petition praying that His Majesty might be graciously pleased to grant a Supplemental Charter to the Hospital was lodged with the Privy Council Office. On January 29th 1951, the

Hospital obtained its Supplemental Charter giving the Council freedom to admit temporary officers and to determine what charges shall 'from time to time' be paid by patients. Royal Assent has thus been given to the policy of the new Hospital.

In the early days at Beaumont House, the Appeals Office was run by an Honorary Secretary, at first Sir George Ogilvie, who was later joined by Lieutenant-Colonel C. I. Shepherd. They worked together effectively but as time passed Harold Wernher and Reggie Macdonald-Buchanan recognized that someone with experience in a separate office from the Hospital was now required. By the greatest good fortune, a retired naval commander came to the Council's notice. He was Sir Jameson Boyd Adams, who had led a colourful and eventful life first as a very young second-in-command of Ernest Shackleton's first Antarctic expedition, then as a highly decorated officer in the First World War, leaving him with the scars of serious wounds.

Adams's methods of raising money were to some minds eccentric and even coarse. He was a great club man: he lived above Pratts and frequented Brooks's and Whites, where he would approach fellow members with the question, 'Got anything for my dump, mate?' It is doubtful whether Sister Agnes would have approved of her Hospital being styled 'the dump' (many doctors have referred to it as such since – and perhaps it is better than 'Aggie's'), but she would undoubtedly have approved of the half million and more he raised during his reign in the Appeals Office.

Adams was universally popular whether at Beaumont Street, in clubland or in the Appeals Office at 175 Piccadilly. His use of invective, in suitable company, was unrestrained; his sartorial style unchanged since Edwardian London: narrow trousers, high-cut waistcoat and curly-brimmed billycock hat, all worn with total unselfconsciousness.

Adams had learned the art of persuasion as the first secretary of King George's Jubilee Trust, to which he had been appointed in 1935. Shortly after his retirement from this post in 1948, he happened to meet an ex-officer friend in St James's Street who was on his way to his gunsmiths with the intention of selling his guns, to which he was greatly attached.

This incident led Adams to recognize that penury affected many retired officers. He himself was not a rich man and had a wife and two children; but when, coincidentally, he was approached by Harold Wernher to head a new Appeals Office for King Edward VII's Hospital he jumped at the opportunity to be of some service to a charitable institution catering especially for indigent officers.

Adams also made good use of the Press for 'planting' and exploiting stories about the Hospital. In the late 1940s and early 1950s the term 'Press Officer' had scarcely been coined. But the House Governor, Sir George Ogilvie, and his successor, as Secretary, the Hon. Mrs Birdwood, did what they could with the Press. In April 1950, for example, a colonel was persuaded to write from the Naval and Military Club (the 'In & Out'):

> Recently I had the misfortune suddenly to be struck down, my condition necessitating an immediate operation. Remembering the publicity you gave to King Edward VII's Hospital for Officers, I contacted it and was admitted within an hour, thus being saved unnecessary anxiety and, possibly, fatal consequences. I am now well on the road to recovery . . .

The colonel continued his letter with an appeal for funds which 'are urgently needed if the splendid work of the Hospital is to continue'.

This was published in *The Times*, and Mrs Birdwood told the officer that 'today's post has brought us a number of enquiries and a donation of £100'.

Notable patients gave the opportunity for their names to be exploited in association with the Hospital. 'Bob' Boothby was one. 'Sir Robert Boothby today begins his convalescence after a month's treatment for heart trouble in that most admirable institution, the King Edward VII's Hospital for Officers,' ran one item in the *Daily Telegraph*.

Field Marshal Viscount Montgomery of Alamein, a figure to reckon with in 1955, could not be bettered as a subject for publicity. The reporters and cameramen swarmed like *paparazzi* of the 1990s. He was photographed with his ward nurse, Matron Saxby, and a party of nurses standing about his bed showing him Press photographs.

After 'Monty', Princess Alexandra, as Colonel-in-Chief of the Durham Light Infantry, was admitted to Sister Agnes's for the removal of a wisdom tooth, and she was followed by HM Queen Elizabeth the Queen Mother, whose association with the Hospital was to be especially close and enduring. She was suffering from an infected appendix, and had to have an urgent operation, as had King Edward VII himself. The King's operation, conducted at Buckingham Palace, had necessitated the postponement of his coronation. In Queen Elizabeth's case it entailed the postponement of a thirty-thousand-mile tour of Canada, Australia and New Zealand, a lesser but still serious inconvenience. All this was the lead story in the newspapers, with many references to 'the Hospital fit for a Queen', and 'Today's Top Hospital'.

HRH the Duke of Kent was the next member of the Royal Family to go to Sister Agnes's but for only a minor operation.

Regimental magazines were a source of publicity which the Hon. Mrs Birdwood and the Appeals Office fully exploited. The May 1951 issue of the *Piffer*, the Journal of the Punjab Frontier Force Officers' Association, opened with this message from the editor:

> I have been rather handicapped in collecting news as on January 17th I was admitted into 'Sister Agnes' desperately ill with pneumonia and my life was only saved by the skill of the doctors and assiduous nursing. I cannot speak too highly of Sister Agnes and I recommend all officers to pay the yearly subscription of £1 which gives them admission at reduced fees; even if they don't benefit themselves they help this grand institution.

This 'grand institution' admitted no fewer than three 'Piffer' generals in as many months, Major-General Inskip and Generals Sir John Brind and Sir Dashwood Strettell. They all testified to the superb efficiency and comfort of 'Sister Agnes's'.

The *Dragon* was the impressive regimental magazine of the East Kent regiment, 'The Buffs', and there was a long, fulsome letter in the April 1951 issue. One paragraph read:

> The object of this letter is to bring to the notice of past and present officers of the regiment the fact that King Edward VII Hospital is again in existence and going very strong, and to point out, borne out by my own recent experience, the many advantages it offers to subscribers.

Citing his own experience, J. F. Whitacre Allen continued:

> I had a very comfortable private ward – quiet, good lighting, excellent Red
> Cross Library, the care and attention could not have been exceeded, but at
> the same time one was treated as a reasonable human being and not unduly
> diciplined or fussed. The food was excellent, well cooked and nicely served.

The article-length letter concluded with a plea that, for their own
benefit as well as the Hospital's, serving and retired Buffs officers
should subscribe to Sister Agnes's.

One more citation, this time by Major G. E. Fenwick MC, in the
St George's Gazette, the magazine of the Royal Northumberland
Fusiliers, read:

> I cannot speak too highly of this Hospital. Having been in a much more
> expensive nursing home last year for an identical operation, I am in a posi-
> tion to judge, and the difference is remarkable. At Sister Agnes's the
> patient comes first and all other considerations are subordinated to that.
> Not only is the skill of the doctors and nurses of the highest order, but
> the whole atmosphere is cheerful and welcoming . . .

In the early years in Beaumont Street the Hospital attracted distinguished visitors as well as patients. The same applied to the opening
ceremonies for extensions to the Hospital and Agnes Keyser House,
the nurses' home, which was almost as impressive as the Hospital itself
on the other side of the street.

One of these early visitors was the Countess Mountbatten of
Burma, who had been closely identified with the Order of St John,
the Red Cross and many forms of humanitarian work during the
recent war. She spent an afternoon in Beaumont Street, and 'was
deeply impressed with all I saw', she wrote the following day.

Perhaps Sister Agnes would not have approved of all this publicity-
seeking, but it was essential to keep the public aware of the existence
of the Hospital and its need for support. It was not always easy to keep
the beds filled and the donations rolling in.

The first full year of the reborn Hospital revealed many shortcom-
ings, but there were good brains on the Council besides those of Harold

Wernher. The first, and most basic, difficulties they had to face were a dearth of patients and a sudden and considerable rise in nursing salaries. Harold suggested that they should ask the administrators of King Edward's Hospital Fund (the King's Fund) for advice. (This fund, like the King Edward VII Hospital in Midhurst, Surrey,* sometimes and understandably was confused with Sister Agnes's.) The King's Fund, which specialized in this area, sent along a committee of two experts in November 1949, and their report was submitted just two months later:

> As a result of the recommendations much reorganization took place and many changes in policy were brought quickly into effect. These changes included a rescaling of fees charged to patients, a reduction and regrading of the nursing staff, the appointment of a Catering Officer and of a full-time accountant, closer control by the Finance Committee over Hospital expenditure . . . Before many months had gone by it was evident that the reorganization, together with a gratifying increase in the number of patients, had succeeded in putting the finances of the Hospital onto a more even keel.

A new wave of self-confidence and good cheer ran through Beaumont House as the advice took effect. The King's Fund compounded this with two gifts in 1950: one of £5,000 and another of £2,500 for specific capital expenses.

The Appeals Office redoubled its efforts, to excellent effect. They found 836 new subscribers, resulting in a rise in annual income, from this source alone, from £5,338 to £7,001. A gift of £1,000 was received 'out of the blue' from serving and retired officers of the famous Indian Cavalry Regiment, the Central India Horse. A report headed 'Income and Expenditure' at the end of 1950 read:

> There has been a great improvement in the financial position of the Hospital. The cost per occupied bed [per week] has been reduced from

---

* Sir Ernest Cassel, Edward VII's banker, lost his wife, and later his only daughter, from tuberculosis. Both he and the King were equally determined to set up a sanatorium for this disease. Cassel opened the fund for its construction with a grant of £200,000.

£42 in 1949 to £29. Income shows a rise under all heads except dividends, some securities having been sold the previous year to meet urgent capital expenditure. On an average throughout the year there were seven more patients in the Hospital each week in 1950 than in 1949, yet the total expenditure for 1950 exceeds that for 1949 by the sum of £1,106 only, of which £500 was for the purchase of new linen.

The official photograph of the opening ceremony of Beaumont House in 1948 features Queen Mary herself, Sir Harold Wernher, Lady Zia Wernher, Sir George Ogilvie, the House Governor, and a diminutive figure in matron's uniform, who is identified as Miss Alice Saxby. She also features in another contemporary photograph, together with her entire nursing staff, all pleasant looking and clearly very competent. Alice Saxby looks as if she has been selected for this important job of Matron because of her physical likeness to Sister Agnes. She certainly shaped her style and manner on what she had learned about her predecessor and founder. 'She was an extraordinary woman,' reported Sir Brian Warren shortly before he died in 1996. He was Resident Medical Officer at Beaumont Street for many years, and had known Sister Agnes and worked closely with Alice Saxby.

> She was determined to model herself on [Sister Agnes] in every respect – voice, attitude. Like Sister Agnes she had curious ideas of grandeur, and managed the Hospital in an autocratic way. She liked titles and I have never seen such a low curtsy, when this was called for – which was as often as possible. She liked titles even more than Sister Agnes did.

Alice Saxby was also as dedicated to her job as her predecessor, and lived for the Hospital.

In an article in *Queen* magazine (8 November 1950) a reference to Matron reads:

> Like the foundress she is very small with a tiny waist accentuated by her sister's uniform. She has curly fair hair crowned with the high frilly bonnet of a St Thomas's Sister which ties in a bow under her chin, a gracious

manner and a soft, low-speaking voice. During the war she was in charge of an officers' wing at Botley Park and nursed many of the first D-Day casualties.

The first post-war Council consisted of seventeen members (today it has thirty-two) with, of course, Sir Harold Wernher as Chairman, the Duke of Gloucester as President and King George VI as Patron. Much of Britain's fighting history was represented among the members, whose number included two senior retired officers from each of the services. Lord Chatfield, then an admiral of the fleet, had been flag captain to Admiral Beatty at the Battle of Jutland and, above the roar of gunfire, had heard his senior comment bitterly, as one more of his battle cruisers blew up, 'There's something wrong with our bloody ships today, Chatfield.'

Admiral Sir Percy Noble had also fought at Jutland, but being a younger officer, distinguished himself later in the Second World War, as Commander-in-Chief of the Western Approaches during critical years of U-boat warfare.

The RAF was represented by two senior officers of great distinction: Marshal of the RAF Sir Edward Ellington, and Air Chief Marshal Sir Douglas Evill. Ellington, at seventy-three the oldest member of the Council, had been a member of the first Air Council in 1918, and had later been appointed Chief of the Air Staff. His administrative experience had been as long and fruitful as anyone on the Hospital's Council. Evill had fought at sea and in the air in the First World War, earning both the Distinguished Service Cross and the Air Force Cross, and had subsequently risen to be Vice-Chief of the Air Staff. 'A most charming and able man,' commented the official air historian.

The two generals on the Council were Sir George Giffard and Otto Lund. Giffard had fought in France in the First World War, had been wounded badly, awarded the DSO and had several times been mentioned in dispatches. In the Second World War he was appointed Commander-in-Chief of the 11th Army Group in South-East Asia. When the youthful Mountbatten came out as supremo the two men clashed from the beginning, most particularly over the issue of whether or not to fight through the monsoon, after which disagreement Mountbatten sacked Giffard.

Lieutenant-General Otto Lund was another survivor of the fighting in Flanders, where he also won the DSO. He was a gunner through and through, and in the Second World War was Major-General first of the Royal Artillery Home Forces and then of 21 Army Group.

Of the medical members of the Council, who also sat on the Medical Committee, were Lord Webb-Johnson (the Chairman) and Sir Cecil Wakeley, both with four decorations after their name. They were, in fact, both surgeons and among the most distinguished of their time. Webb-Johnson had a CBE and DSO from the First World War, besides having been mentioned in dispatches three times. He had subsequently been appointed Queen Mary's surgeon, and among his long list of posts, he had become vice-president and consulting surgeon to Middlesex Hospital. He was also associated with Manchester University and became a member of the Court of Examiners, Royal College of Surgeons. Webb-Johnson was particularly known for his treatment of cancer, as well as typhoid and para-typhoid fevers. Now seventy years old, he was the second oldest member of the Council, but was still as sharp as he had ever been in the 1920s and 1930s.

Cecil Wakeley was Webb-Johnson's junior by twelve years. His war service had been in the Royal Navy in both world wars, during which he had risen to the rank of Surgeon Rear-Admiral. He, too, was much concerned with cancer surgery, and acted as consulting surgeon to King's College Hospital. He was also chairman of the Council of the Imperial Cancer Research Fund for a number of years. Wakeley was an examiner in surgery to no fewer than seven universities, London, Cambridge, Durham, Sheffield, Glasgow, Wales and Dublin.

The 1950 report concludes:

> The welfare of the patients is the first consideration of the Council and the year has seen some notable additions made towards their comfort and well-being. A telephone system which allows the use of individual receivers to all patients in single rooms has been installed. Ward patients share a line.
>
> The management of the library [once Fanny Keyser's responsibility] has

been taken over by the Red Cross and that organization loaned the Hospital many new books as part of its library service.

Every effort is being made to keep down the cost of treatment to patients. Up to the present it has not been possible to eliminate 'extras' from the patients' bills, but if the financial position continues to improve as it has done over the past year, the reduction of additional charges to patients will be a first call on the resources of the Hospital.

The formation in 1951 of a Consulting Staff for the Hospital, with fees to be charged in accordance with the patients' means, will go far towards reducing the cost of an illness to individual patients.

CHAPTER 10

Better Facilities for the Nurses

AS THE INSPIRATION and driving force behind the rebirth of the Hospital at Beaumont House, Sir Harold Wernher maintained a firm hand on the tiller during its formative stage. At the same time, despite his advancing years (he was born in January 1893), he maintained his business interests in Electrolux and Plessey and other companies; in property, especially London theatres; and in Bermuda, where he had built the mighty Bermudiana hotel. Horse breeding and racing still attracted him.

Harold's tall, austere, straight-backed figure with the military moustache he had worn since young manhood, continued to be a familiar sight about the City, the race tracks and the social events of the season. He kept fit and busy, his mind as acute as it had always been.

The year 1951, the third full year in the reborn Hospital's life, was one of consolidation. The report declared that:

> It is now a fully functioning, modern, specialized unit for the surgical and medical treatment of officers and ex-officers of the three Services. There is also the evidence of many of Sister Agnes's old patients to testify that the spirit and traditions of the old Hospital live on in the new.

There were, however, two changes of importance. The first concerned the appointment of a consultant staff, similar to that appointed in 1904. This panel of consultants was dropped when the Hospital returned from Grosvenor Gardens to 17 Grosvenor Crescent in 1919. No reason for this was given at the time, but now King Edward's Hospital Fund, who were benign advisers always hovering in the corridors, considered that the appointment of a consulting staff was necessary 'if the professional fees charged to patients were to bear some relation to the bed charges of the Hospital'.

As before, the relatively modest fees expected of these consultants were, it was thought, likely to be offset for them by the accruing prestige of being on the staff list.

The medical members of the Council therefore selected a list of twenty-seven surgeons and physicians who would be invited to participate. All but one gladly and willingly agreed, their fees to be charged on a scale 'to be based on the patient's income, the charges to be assessed and recovered by the Secretary'. The system no longer applies.

As anticipated when the Council, in the form of Sir George Ogilvie and Harold Wernher, had made the decision to buy the Beaumont Street wreck in 1948, there would necessarily be an ongoing need for more beds and more space, especially for a nurses' home. The most urgent internal need was the construction of a dispensary. Advice on this was provided by the dispenser of the Hospital of St John and St Elizabeth in St John's Wood. Messrs Boots also offered advice, and the dispensary, a tremendous economy and convenience, opened for full service on 1 September 1951. At the same time, of equally urgent need was a large refrigerated room for the storage of food. This was constructed, without any trouble, on the fourth floor of the building.

But it was staff accommodation that most seriously preoccupied the Executive Committee, the comfort of staff being of equal importance with the comfort and well-being of patients. First, extensive alterations were carried out to the two adjoining houses, numbers 5 and 6 Beaumont Street. A mews flat in Devonshire Close was also acquired.

The most formidable undertaking, however, concerned the bombed site on the other side of the Hospital, number 7 Beaumont Street. It must be filled in! 'The new building,' ran the report, 'will provide the urgently needed additional patients' rooms, a new and improved bed lift, and the requisite staff accommodation for the enlarged Hospital.'

If, at this time and subsequently, it appears that the de Walden Estate, which held the ground leases of the property in this part of Marylebone, were swift and pliant in dealing with requests from King Edward VII's Hospital, it is worth pointing out that Lord Howard de Walden was a horse racing crony of both Wernher and Macdonald-Buchanan.

The Honorary Appeals Secretary, Adams, and the House and Finance Committee, were hard-pressed, with all this ambitious expansion, to keep the finances on an even keel. Adams, in particular, was singled out in the Annual Report – 'His work for the Hospital has been so unremitting and so fruitful.'

With the permission of the King, Adams masterminded the writing and production of a book, *Our Way of Life*, with contributions by distinguished public men, and a lunch at St James's Palace to mark its publication. He also organized the presentation of a performance of *Present Laughter* by the Stock Exchange Dramatic Society at the Scala Theatre shortly before Christmas, the proceeds of which helped to make this a record year for the Appeals Office, which could, as well, report a steady increase in receipts from subscriptions and donations.

This was all good news, but none of the cost of the extension was included in these figures. This led Harold Wernher to sound a cautionary note – in capital letters: 'AS THE COST OF BUILDING THIS EXTENSION WILL BE IN THE NEIGHBOURHOOD OF £40,000* IT WILL BE REALISED THAT THE COUNCIL IS FACED WITH A FORMIDABLE FINANCIAL TASK.'

On 6 February 1952, the Hospital's Patron, King George VI, died. In sharp contrast to the previous female monarch, her great-great grandmother, Queen Victoria, who was at Kensington Palace when she became Queen, the heir to the throne was in deepest Africa. She returned by air to a solemn welcome. Elizabeth Longford described her arrival at Heathrow:

---

* Approximately £500,000 in today's money.

'Shall I go down alone?' she asked her relatives who had boarded the plane to greet her – the Mountbattens and her uncle the Duke of Gloucester.

The eighteen-year-old Victoria had met her Archbishop, Lord Chamberlain and the late King's physician for the first time '*alone*', having deliberately freed herself from her mother's hand in order to do so. Now Prince Philip stepped back of his own accord. The slight black figure of the young Queen, strong in her loneliness and the chivalry it aroused, walked slowly down the gangway into her new life.[1]

Anthony Eden was to remember vividly the Queen's arrival. 'The sight of that young figure in black,' he wrote in 1960, 'coming through the door of the aircraft, standing there poised for a second before descending . . . is a poignant memory.'[2]

There to greet her, besides Anthony Eden, the Foreign Secretary, were her Prime Minister, Winston Churchill, and the Leader of the Opposition, Clement Attlee.

At the meeting of the Hospital's Council in October 1952, Harold Wernher made the following announcement:

It is my duty to express to you, Sir [i.e. the President, the Duke of Gloucester] on behalf of the Council of the Hospital our deep sympathy on the death of our Patron, His late Majesty King George VI. I need only say that his loss was felt keenly by all connected with the Hospital, as it was by the nation as a whole.

It is with pleasure that I am able to announce that Her Majesty the Queen has been graciously pleased to accept the Patronage of the Hospital. Her Majesty is the fifth Sovereign of the Royal Family to honour this Hospital thus, and the Council, with humble duty, desire to record their deep gratitude for the honour which Her Majesty has conferred upon them.

Another sad royal event was the death of Queen Mary on 24 March 1953. Although she had not visited Beaumont Street as frequently as she used to call at 17 Grosvenor Crescent, partly because of her age and problems of mobility, there were still members of the staff who could recall her trips from Buckingham Palace for a cigarette and a cup of tea with Sister Agnes, and she had been closely connected with the Hospital for many years.

To offset this loss, their Patron was crowned a few weeks later. The corridors of the Hospital were decorated as if for Christmas, almost every patient listened to the ceremony on a portable wireless, and in some of the wards, and in the nurses' sitting-room, television sets showed the wonder of the ancient coronation ceremony.

By August 1952 building had begun on the Hospital extension. It was decided that because of the importance and size – to say nothing of the cost – of this development its construction should be supervised by a Building Sub-Committee under the chairmanship of Marshal of the RAF Sir Edward Ellington. The aim was to complete it in about eighteen months, or early in 1954. Harold Wernher told the Council:

> The extension will provide much needed additional single rooms for patients, a physiotherapy treatment room, accommodation for the staff required, and will allow for an eventual increase in size and scope of the existing X-ray and operating theatre suites. One sixth of the total cost will be for a new and improved bed lift to the Hospital, of the latest construction and design . . .

Harold was anxious that this extension should be completed free from the burden of debt. A Building Fund was therefore opened and all concerned made an extra effort, especially among the potentially large contributors, such as from King George's Fund for Sailors, which gave £3,000, the ever-generous City Guilds, and the old friends, the King's Fund, which promised £2,500. A further £2,500 was received from an unexpected quarter, the British War Relief Society of America. There was a ceremonial presentation of the cheque to the Duke and Duchess of Gloucester at St James's Palace. The biggest contribution of all was £5,000 from the Public Trustee.

The importance of Adams's Appeals Office was signified by its removal to 15 Ormond Yard, Duke of York Street, where it had vastly improved accommodation and increased space.

The year 1953 was one of controlled chaos. The sound of builders at work was ceaseless, and the already crowded Beaumont Street was congested further by builders' lorries. It was not a restful period for either patients or staff.

Early in the year a request was made to their friends and ever obliging advisers, the King's Fund, for guidance on the general internal arrangements of the Hospital in view of the imminent completion of number 7. It was decided, in view of the radical nature of the Fund's report, to close the Hospital entirely for the last six weeks of the year while internal building and decorating took place and number 7 was dovetailed into the existing building. The report read:

> As a result of the combined operations to build an extension and to improve the existing building, the new Hospital now has ten additional single rooms for patients, a new bed lift, a physiotherapy treatment room and a medical and subscription room. The ward floors have been improved by the construction of nurses' duty rooms, additional bathrooms and lavatories. The catering floor has been redesigned to give larger pantry and trolley loading areas and improved ventilation in the kitchen. Perhaps the greatest improvement is that of the operating theatre suite; by taking in the area which was the matron's flat, the suite has been doubled in size and will now provide a surgical milieu of the highest order.

Besides Harold Wernher, the other figure most responsible for the planning and successful conclusion of all this rebuilding was Lord Webb-Johnson. Alfred Edward Webb-Johnson was a most remarkable figure in the medical world at this time, holding a great number of appointments, including that of surgeon to Queen Mary before she died. Born in 1880, the son of a doctor in Stoke-on-Trent, he soon made a name for himself as a surgeon specializing in cancer. (He later wrote a notable book entitled *Pride and Prejudice in the Treatment of Cancer*.) He became consulting surgeon to the British Expeditionary Force in France in 1914, was mentioned in dispatches and was awarded the DSO. In London he was associated with the Middlesex Hospital and the Royal Hospital, Chelsea. When Beaumont Street opened in 1948, Webb-Johnson was persuaded to chair the Medical Committee. By the conclusion of the 1953 rebuilding, he and his committee had

not only brought about several major improvements in the medical services to the Hospital but [had] also given much valuable guidance in the
replanning equipment of the operating theatre suite and of the medical
fittings to the ward floors . . .

Lord Webb-Johnson was also personally responsible for the agreement with the Middlesex Hospital by which it would carry out the
more complicated X-ray examinations on patients of King Edward
VII's. As a result of this and other voluntary work, Webb-Johnson
was awarded the Knight Grand Cross of the Royal Victorian Order
in the 1954 New Year's Honours. Unfortunately his health began to
decline soon after this, although he continued almost to the end to
serve on the Council. He died on 28 May 1958. He is remembered
with affection by members of his favourite club, the Garrick, where
in the evening he sat at dinner at the head of the long table, just as,
in an earlier time, Henry Irving sat, chattering away to left and to
right.

A problem that would not go away was that of the long-stay elderly
patient. The report read:

It is not possible for the Hospital to block beds indefinitely with patients
who require in the main a permanent 'home'. Few of these patients can
afford the fees of expensive private nursing homes and the accommodation offered by other institutions free, or at very low fees, is not usually of
a kind which would bring contentment and peace of mind to a chron-
ically ill retired officer. The Hospital does what it can for these sad cases
by caring for them for short periods and in searching for permanent
homes of a suitable type.

Thanks to exceptional efforts by the Appeals Office and some timely
and unexpected gifts, including £5,000 from the American
Ambulance Society of Great Britain, which eight years after the
conclusion of the Second World War was going into voluntary
liquidation, all financial targets were met.

Within a few months of the completion of the additional wing,

Harold Wernher concluded his annual report with these words:

> The thoughts of the Council turn now to the future, and to the further rehabilitation of the old building; to the need for a larger nurses' home and more staff accommodation and in due course to a possible increase in the size of the Hospital.

Clearly, the Chairman had no intention of giving the Council an easy life. Harold was, after all, a man of enterprise. On its fiftieth birthday as Sister Agnes's, the Hospital could boast that it mustered among its medical and surgical staff the aristocracy of the medical profession, although, like Sister Agnes, Matron Alice Saxby did not allow them to get above themselves.

Sir Archibald McIndoe's name as plastic surgeon was known outside the grateful circle of the RAF and other services who were treated by him for burns at the Queen Victoria Plastic and Jaw Injury Centre at East Grinstead. Born and educated in New Zealand, McIndoe had come to England after completing his medical training at Otago. Long before the Second World War he was regarded as one of the top plastic surgeons in Britain, and his work at East Grinstead, particularly on burned Battle of Britain pilots like Richard Hillary, resulted in popular acclaim, and no honour brought him more pleasure than that of Life Presidency of the Guinea Pig Club – i.e. aircrew who had saved themselves by bailing out. On a strictly professional level he had been President of the Association of Plastic Surgeons.

Among the orthopaedic surgeons were Henry Osmond-Clarke, later knighted, Cecil Fleming and Ronald Furlong. Of the eight general surgeons, perhaps Sir Cecil Wakeley Bt., senior consulting surgeon to the Royal Navy, was the best known. Julian Taylor CBE was a University College Hospital man though subsequently he had worked at the Universities of Khartoum and Singapore. In the First World War he had served with the 85th Field Ambulance and later was invited to serve on the Council of the Royal College of Surgeons.

Sir Clement Price Thomas KCVO had enjoyed a fine 1914–18 war record in the RAMC at Gallipoli, and in Macedonia and Palestine. Thoracic surgery was his special subject. In this capacity he was in turn consultant in thoracic surgery to the RAF and Army. Among his other credits was honorary consulting surgeon to Westminster Hospital and joint lecturer in surgery at Westminster Hospital Medical School.

The surgeon–apothecary in 1955 was Brian Warren, who remained in this role until 1993, collecting a knighthood among other honours on the way. Warren had been MO to the Grenadier Guards from 1943 and a civilian doctor at Wellington Barracks.

At King Edward VII's he worked closely with Alice Saxby and on the whole got on well with her. When Warren's great friend, Ted Heath, the future premier, succumbed to jaundice, the Hospital was full, but Warren ingratiated himself with her: 'He's a famous politician, Alice, you must have a bed for my friend.' And she did.

Warren today describes relations between Matron Saxby and the Secretary (then Lady Birdwood), two strong characters, as 'an armed alliance'.

Harold Wernher had known Lord Mountbatten for many years, and the two families were closely linked. Mountbatten's elder brother, George Milford Haven, had married Nada, Zia Wernher's sister. Harold used to talk about his hospital work when at Broadlands, where he often stayed with Zia. This aroused the interest not only of Mountbatten, but of his wife, Edwina, who had devoted much of her life to hospital charities and St John Ambulance work.

Harold also told them about King Edward VII's Hospital, and his chairmanship in succession to Sister Agnes. The Mountbattens had of course heard about the reopening of the Hospital in Beaumont Street. When Harold recited the names of some of the members of the Council, Mountbatten's competitive sense, always well tuned, was aroused and he put himself forward as a candidate for membership, too. Whether Harold welcomed this notion is not known, but it is fair to conclude that he must have had some reservations: Mountbatten tended to be dominant at any gathering, and at present all the members were very compatible, a good team in fact.

Mountbatten was duly elected a Council member in 1955, at the same time as the new Chief of the Imperial General Staff, General Sir Gerald Templer. This was not very timely. Templer and Mountbatten were old antagonists. Their last disagreement had been over what

Templer (and others, including Churchill) believed was Mountbatten's overenthusiasm for handing back India and many colonies to their people.

There would, however, be no antagonism between Mountbatten and another distinguished member, Admiral of the Fleet Sir Arthur Power, one of Mountbatten's commanders in the wartime Far East Command. Mountbatten described him as 'an old friend' and 'a most loyal friend to me'.

In the context of this Hospital meeting the two Admirals of the Fleet recalled the critical wartime meeting round Mountbatten's sickbed after he had succumbed to amoebic dysentery.

Mountbatten had also had trouble in the past with another Council member, the venerable Admiral Chatfield. One particular dispute concerned the Invergordon Mutiny in 1931. This was caused by the sudden introduction of pay cuts in the fleet because the nation was going broke. Mountbatten was in the Mediterranean at the time as Fleet Wireless Officer under Chatfield, the Commander-in-Chief. Signallers were always first with the news and Mountbatten considered that the only way to avoid a mutiny in the Mediterranean was to cut off all wireless communication and disperse the fleet. This suggestion from a junior officer did not in the least please the Admiral, who had complete trust in his men. But Mountbatten argued his case so convincingly (he said later) that Chatfield agreed to follow the suggestion. Ever after, when the subject of the Invergordon Mutiny came up Mountbatten claimed that he had saved the Mediterranean Fleet single-handed.

Now, twenty-five years later, he was to sit round the same table as Chatfield, but Mountbatten was no longer a lieutenant-commander; he was an admiral, too, and had himself commanded the Mediterranean Fleet.

But, like the other Council members, Mountbatten now bent his mind to the parochial matters of the Hospital, and the first subject to which they turned their attention was staff accommodation. As Mountbatten and the other admirals knew, good accommodation for the lower deck was the first requirement for a happy ship. Many of the staff were accommodated in two run-down houses, numbers 5 and 6 Beaumont Street. A Staff Accommodation Sub-Committee was therefore set up under the chairmanship of Sir Edward Ellington. As a one-time Chief of Air Staff, he was well equipped to deal with the problems that lay ahead. The first of these was finance. Luck was on Ellington's side.

> On 1 April the Hospital was honoured with a visit from Mr Clark Minor, Chairman of the War Relief Society of America, accompanied by Mrs Minor and Mrs Rex Benson. The visitors were shown over the building and at the conclusion of the tour the Chairman indicated that the project to build a nurses' home might be of interest to the Society. A month later Sir Robert Appleby, the Vice-Chairman, came to the Hospital with Mrs Benson and confirmed the intention of the Society to make a very substantial gift towards the cost of the new Home, which is estimated at about £80,000.

Harold Wernher had for some time had his eye on a bombed and cleared site in Beaumont Street almost opposite the Hospital. Negotiations were now put in hand with the de Walden Estate, and were concluded swiftly and satisfactorily in a matter of weeks, perhaps at Doncaster races? The Hospital's architects drew up a design which included thirty-nine bedsitting rooms and two self-contained flats, estimated time for completion, spring 1957. Mountbatten, ever the hustler, approved of that.

The building and furnishing of the new nurses' home – to be known as Agnes Keyser House – was 'not without setbacks and anxiety', as could have been anticipated. But on 21 November 1957, it was ready for the opening ceremony, to be performed by Queen Elizabeth the Queen Mother, who has always taken the keenest interest in the Hospital. In fact, after the death of Queen Mary, she was the most involved member of the Royal Family – excepting only the Duke of Gloucester, who remained as President. Her Majesty and her brother-in-law arrived together, and Beaumont Street was closed to through traffic.

More than two hundred guests attended the ceremony, and to underline the continuity of the Hospital since Sister Agnes's time, three of her old Sisters, including one aged eighty-seven, were among those presented to Her Majesty. The speeches included that of Mr Clark Minor, who had flown over from New York with his wife. Because they and their Committee were responsible for the original grant, the very least that could be done to acknowledge this was to have a notice carved in the entrance hall, reading:

> This Home for Nurses, the gift of the British War Relief Society of America and other friends of King Edward VII's Hospital for Officers, was opened by Her Majesty Queen Elizabeth the Queen Mother on November 21st, 1957.

After this was unveiled, tea was served and a tour of the home undertaken.

The year 1957 was one of records for the Hospital: the number of in-patients admitted was 923 compared with 849 the previous year; salaries and wages were up from £7,900 to £9,000, and so on, but all increases were commensurate with the increase in patients treated and number of beds. To offset this increase in expenditure, donations were up from £6,500 to £10,200, the first time five figures had been reached. As for income for 1957, annual subscriptions totalled £17,838 and included £100 each from the Queen and the Duke of Gloucester, £250 from the Wernher Charitable Trust, and 'others' including tax recovered on deeds of Covenant, £17,188.

In terms of grants, the ever-helpful King's Fund headed the list with £1,000, and the Army Benevolent Fund chipped in with £450. Smaller donations totalled £10,187, also an all-time record.

Other income came from patients' fees, totalling £22,545, which was £3,000 up on the previous year, while investments totalled another £3,000. Total income was £56,744.

There were many reasons for this satisfactory position at the end of 1957. Records were broken, too, by Sir Jameson Adams, the Honorary Appeals Secretary, whose zeal was unsurpassed. Wernher said of him, 'Our debt has reached a stage at which we saw no hope of ever repaying it. His efforts have enabled us to go forward, unhampered by debt, with the enlargement and improvement of the Hospital . . .'

Reference was also made to some of his subsidiary fund-raising activities, like the BBC's 'Week's Good Cause' appeal that year. It was made by Captain Anthony Kimmins RN, the much admired playwright, whose most recent success was *Smiley*. The appeal brought in just short of £2,000. This was followed by a single performance at the Savoy Theatre of *Free as Air*, in the presence of HRH Princess Alexandra. It was a sell-out, and £3,000 was made for the Hospital.

Harold Wernher and the members of the Council were in a buoyant mood at the end of 1957, having accomplished so much during the year. But there was more to come. Under the will of Mr Alexander Levy a bequest was to be made for the rebuilding of numbers 5 and 6 Beaumont Street, the run-down and recently vacated nurses' quarters. The Trustees of this bequest were the King's Fund, and it was from these old friends of the Hospital that the glad news was received. The sum involved was little short of half a million pounds. But there was a curious condition attached to this bequest, which would have attracted a lot of unfavourable attention forty years later. The Trust laid down that patients must be members of the 'educated middle classes'. Since no sex was mentioned it was, therefore, implicit that women and children as well as men must be admitted to the new extension wing, *and* they would have to be well educated.

Harold Wernher concluded his report for the year:

The House and Finance Committee considered the offer at a meeting held on 4th December, 1958, and decided to accept the offer provisionally, and a scheme for submission to the King's Fund will now be prepared. The Hospital thus enters the year 1958 with a new, complex, but immensely stimulating project before it.

That was how Harold liked it!

CHAPTER II

Bigger and Bigger

LTHOUGH WORK STARTED on the Levy Wing in August 1958 and, amazingly, was completed in October 1959, this new wing was one of the chief concerns of the Council in the early part of the following decade. At the AGM in May 1960, Harold Wernher 'was able to report that the wing had already been well assimilated into the day to day running of the Hospital and that there were no medico-administrative problems . . .'

The Duke of Gloucester had been unable to attend this AGM but he made a special visit a month later, on 10 June 1960, to inspect the Levy Wing. Also present on this occasion were those who had been most closely concerned with the birth and completion of the whole enterprise, including the executors of Mr Levy's will, the Chief Charity Commissioner, and two representatives of the King's Fund.

With charges of only fifteen guineas a week for maintenance, and fees charged by physicians and surgeons kept as low as possible, it should have been no surprise that a shortage of beds in the new wing soon became critical. This was resolved by the Medical Committee, which ruled that only patients placed by their general practitioners under the care of a member of the medical and surgical staff would be admitted.

In that same year of 1960 there was a shuffling of the Chiefs of Staff Council members. Admiral Sir Caspar John (Augustus John's brother) took the place of Admiral Sir Charles Lambe, who, alas, died soon after his resignation. Representing the RAF was Air Chief Marshal Sir Thomas Pike who had been appointed Chief of Air Staff in succession to Marshal of the RAF Sir Dermot Boyle.

The year 1961 marked a new level of pace and activity. Harold Wernher described it as 'a busy and successful year' with beds full to capacity and without interference from any building operations. 'It has above all,' he continued, 'been a year of unprecedented response to appeals for voluntary income, in spite of the serious illness towards the end of the year of Commander Sir Jameson Adams, the much loved and admired Honorary Appeals Secretary.' Perhaps he had worked too hard for the good of his health, or perhaps it was the old enemy, age, for he was over eighty. Appeals brought in more individual gifts than ever before, besides the annual gifts from regular benefactors like King George's Fund for Sailors, the Godfrey Mitchell Charitable Trust, the Sir James Knott Trust, and various City Guilds.

The RAF Central Fund was another generous benefactor, and the RAF additionally allotted Battle of Britain Sunday for the Hospital's 'Week's Good Cause' BBC appeal. The speaker was none other than Jimmy Edwards DFC, whose ample moustache and ready wit made him one of variety's favourite figures, notable especially for his playing of the euphonium. He had been a patient at the Hospital, and now his appeal brought in a flood of donations and letters.

The Duke of Gloucester in his presidential address the following year, 1962, reported the highest ever number of patients, and strongly hinted at the need for yet further expansion, 'if we are to avoid a reputation for being a hospital in which no patient can be offered a bed in an emergency'.

But the news that dominated and darkened the thoughts of the Council, and indeed everybody associated with the Hospital, was the death in September 1962 of 'the Mate' – Commander Sir Jameson Adams KCVO CBE DSO. Adams 'had been an outstanding figure since he joined the Hospital in 1949, and until the day of his death worked unceasingly in its service'. As members of Whites and Brooks's bore witness, 'he possessed a magic touch for money-raising, born of a conviction that the special care of the retired officer in illness was a paramount duty of all who had benefited from that officer's courage and valour in time of war'.

Following a long obituary in *The Times* there was a further tribute from one of his closest admirers which concluded:

> For integrity of mind and for the gift for friendship he can have had few rivals. And if in appropriate company his use of somewhat crude invective was unrestrained, there was no one who could fail to recognize in him both a great gentleman and a great Christian.

The Council decided that a memorial window to Adams should be designed, and this was unveiled by the Duke of Gloucester the following year.

Perhaps it was significant that the Council now decided it required two Appeals Secretaries to replace Adams: they were Admiral Sir Alan Scott-Moncrieff, who had commanded a flotilla of destroyers during the stickiest period of the war, earning a DSO and bar; and Humphrey Bevan, who had been an accountant.

Meanwhile, in his usual swift, decisive style, Harold Wernher opened further negotiations with the Howard de Walden Estate, the ground landlords for the area. Like many large London estates they could be tough to deal with, but they had been tolerant and anxious to please the Hospital, its name and connections calling for a certain deference, quite apart from any horse-racing connections. Wernher learned that the leases of adjoining properties in Beaumont Street and Devonshire Street were shortly due to expire. Before the year was out, a rebuilding lease for the two properties was successfully negotiated with the de Walden Estate, to take effect on the expiry of the current lease in 1970.

A further loss to the Hospital was Lord Evans, the Chairman of the Medical Committee and therefore the senior physician. He died in the Hospital to which he had given so much in October 1963, and the tragedy was compounded by the death of his widow, Helen, also in the Hospital, a few weeks later. Lord Evans was succeeded by Sir Arthur Porritt, who held that responsible post until 1966.

In that same year of 1963, the Prime Minister, Harold Macmillan, was admitted as an emergency patient, qualifying as an officer on the Western Front in the First World War. He underwent a major operation two days later, but the strains and stresses of his long premiership were beginning to tell, and when the Queen visited him in Beaumont Street, he used the occasion to offer his resignation. A plaque commemorates the event today.

The accommodation of important people at the Hospital had, as we have seen, the benefit of drawing public attention to it. But the presence of reporters and photographers in Beaumont Street also tended to give it a hint of élitism. Further, it had the equally unfortunate consequence of suggesting that it was a rich person's Hospital and was therefore rich in funds. Not only had the Queen been seen visiting her Prime Minister, but in February 1964, Her Majesty Queen Elizabeth the Queen Mother was admitted for an appendix operation. This was the first of several visits. Her affection and admiration for King Edward VII's Hospital is widely known, and her private secretary wrote to this historian, 'As you know, Queen Elizabeth has herself been a patient on a number of occasions and Her Majesty is full of praise for the standard of nursing care and most appreciative of the kindness and consideration shown to her.'

The Queen Mother on this occasion remained for two weeks and made a speedy and complete recovery.

Harold Wernher in his 1964 report wrote of it being 'an interesting though in some respects a rather difficult year'. The first difficulty was of a structural nature. The original nursing home from which the Hospital emerged had been soundly built – enough to withstand the worst that the *Luftwaffe* could throw at it. But the floors were of wood block, very fashionable in the 1930s, and had by now reached the end of their life. Their replacement by boards would entail an unacceptable disturbance. Therefore it was decided to close down altogether for some seven weeks in August and September while this work was carried out.

What the Hospital needed at this time was a good Press officer. For the second time in the year an announcement was issued without proper thought for the consequences. The Council had decided on a fundamental change of policy. As we have seen, from 1 January 1965 only the Hospital's recognized consultant staff would be permitted to attend patients. The reason for this restriction, which was taken with the utmost reluctance, was that it had become urgently necessary to impose some limitation on the over-whelming number of specialists attending patients . . . The pressure on the beds had become such that it was rarely possible to admit a patient in an emergency and the waiting list for entry was extending from weeks to months.

Many distinguished specialists had to be told that they could no longer bring their patients to King Edward VII's, and it was treated as an affront by some patients who had been so treated in the past and might wish to do so again.

The announcement of this change of policy 'was misrepresented in certain Press reports causing distress and bewilderment to a great number of officers who had subscribed to the Hospital for many years . . .' A sound, experienced Press officer knows that an announce-ment should be worded so that it cannot be misrepresented. 'A correcting statement has been published,' concluded this item lamely, 'and it is now hoped that the reasons for the change have been made clear.' But the damage had been done.

The more charitable conclusion to all this is that the Hospital had become a victim of its own success.

The year 1964 was not all difficulties, however, and there is an amusing anecdote involving two ex-officers of roughly equal eccentricity who were glad to make use of Sister Agnes's facilities at the time. Randolph Churchill went in to have a lung removed. His biographer, Alan Brien, recounted:

Death itself did not frighten him . . . It was a treat to see him refuse to be reduced to a vegetable, as most people are, ticking off the eminent sur-geons for talking about doctor's orders. 'I'm paying. It's my lung. I give the orders. I take advice, but I give the orders.' He instructed the formid-able matron [Alice Saxby] on how to make a decent cup of tea. He insisted on seeing what had been removed before allowing it to be disposed of. 'It was rather nasty-looking, really,' he told me. 'Like a fat mutton chop you wouldn't even give to the dog. Well rid of that, I'd say.'[1]

This operation precluded Evelyn Waugh from going in for an examination in case he met his old enemy. Instead, the operation led to one happy consequence, as described by Waugh in his diaries:

> It was announced that the trouble was not malignant. Seeing Ed Stanley [Baron Stanley of Alderley] in Whites on my way to Rome, I remarked that it was a typical triumph of modern science to find the only part of Randolph that was not malignant and remove it. Ed repeated this to Randolph whom I met on my return from Rome, again in Whites. He looked so pale and feeble and was so breathless that we there and then made up our estrangement of some twelve years.[2]

The Hospital may have lacked a Press officer but both the chief superintendent and the engineer, both of whom had given good service over many years, resigned and had to be replaced. New patient comforts included a shower on every floor, installed at the request of the Hospital's royal patient, HM the Queen Mother. Perhaps she had also decided that the primitive wireless earphones were not up to scratch for the 1960s, and everyone brought their transistors with them anyway. So the earphones were torn out. As for new-fangled television, as we have seen, wards were wired up with sockets leading to a central aerial at the time of the Coronation. And now more and more patients brought in rented sets.

Improved comforts for patients were matched by new premises for the Appeals Office. Mr Bevan had found it necessary to resign as joint Honorary Appeals Secretary, but Admiral Scott-Moncrieff decided that he could manage with his present staff and the Assistant Appeals Secretary, the diligent and admirable Mrs Margaret 'Peggy' Phillips.

Another figure now enters the Appeals Office scene: Mr Reginald Graham. Mr Graham was a businessman from the North of England who had decided to sell his successful company, move south and use his time and the proceeds from this sale for charitable purposes. The first time his name is mentioned in connection with the Hospital is the offer by him and his wife to design, lay out and produce the brochure for the Extension Appeal Fund. It so happened that this coincided with the termination of the lease of the existing Appeals Office. Reginald Graham stepped in and offered the ground floor and basement of a Georgian house he owned, 6 Buckingham Place, SW1, rent free.

The move took place within weeks. Never had it been such a hectic time for the Appeals Secretary and his staff, and the Council recorded special thanks for all the work they put in. It was somewhat ironic that almost at the same time they were informed that the original target of £300,000 for the extension cost had been increased to £350,000. They began to feel like a party of climbers on a scree slope – 'one step forward and two back'.

One of the Appeals Department's greatest responsibilities was the organizing of a reception in June 1965 for six hundred guests at St James's Palace, at which the Queen Mother and other members of the Royal Family would be present. Lady Zia Wernher was responsible for sending out the invitations. On the day, she and Harold received the guests, assisted by Sir Gerald Templer, now Field Marshal, and Lady Templer.

The purpose of this grand reception was to celebrate the Wolfson Foundation's promise of £100,000, which ensured that the final figure would be reached. Sir Isaac himself presented the first instalment of this money, a cheque for £20,000, to the Queen Mother at this event.

Sister Agnes would not have approved of all the publicity surrounding this reception, but the Council rightly took the view that when a sum of money approaching half a million is required, such fastidiousness has to be forgotten.

Another excitement was reported at the Council's AGM:

Field Marshal Lord Montgomery of Alamein, an old friend and patient of the Hospital, presented us with the Union Flag flown by him on Lüneburg Heath at the surrender of the German Army in 1945, together with a signed photograph of the event. It was the Field Marshal's wish that the flag be sold to raise funds for the extension appeal. The Macdonald-Buchanan Charitable Trust, through the generosity of Sir Reginald and the Hon. Lady Macdonald-Buchanan, bought the flag for the Hospital and it is now framed with the photograph and hung in the entrance hall.

The main activity and subject for discussion during 1966 was the Extension Appeal Fund. Only the year before the Hospital was confident that with the Wolfson grant of £100,000 they were home and dry, but in his own inimitable style Wernher was determined to take things further. It was now decided to rebuild 37a Devonshire Street at the same time as the extension. This was to provide individual flats for senior nursing staff. We have no record of the minutes of the meeting at which the decision was made; but we can legitimately presume that Harold Wernher used one decisive argument in favour of his proposal: Sister Agnes would have approved. Included in the figure of £150,000 for this work was 'a fine new operating theatre'.

At the same time, after meeting many times during the year, the Extension Planning Sub-Committee came out in favour of a continuation of the basic existing design of bay windows with ornamental lead 'aprons'. Anyone viewing the Hospital from across the street today, with the completed extension well matured and all but indistinguishable from the original rebuilt Hospital, must agree that the Committee were absolutely right in their decision.

Meanwhile, the date of the lease had been advanced by three years and it was hoped that the rebuilding could begin in May 1967.

Seven firms had been invited to tender for this large undertaking. The lowest, which was in the region of £450,000, was that of Holland & Hannen and Cubitts (Southern) Ltd; it was accepted. The first builders' lorries turned up at the end of May, and by mid-June the work was well under way. It was still on schedule six months later, but by then it had become clear that, as feared, for the final four months the Hospital would have to be totally closed down, 'in order to co-ordinate the engineering services'. This would be an immensely complicated and demanding undertaking. Harold Wernher confirmed:

> The closure, the need for which was much regretted by the Council, was in itself a major undertaking, requiring many months of planning. Arrangements had to be made for the admission elsewhere of potential patients; for those members of the staff who would seek re-employment when the Hospital re-opened; and for the storage, disposal or overhaul of some 1,300 items of major equipment.

A further complication was the falling behind by the builders of the scheduled programme in the autumn. All building work was to have been completed by the end of November, but it now became clear that no patients could be admitted before April 1969.

Amidst this tumult of committee work and planning there occurred the deaths of two prominent Council members, Lieutenant-Colonel Sir George Ogilvie and Rear Admiral Sir Philip Clarke. Ogilvie had been House Governor in Sister Agnes's time (appointed in 1938), had supervised the move to Luton Hoo on the outbreak of war, had kept an eye on the funds when the Hospital was closed and then bombed, and was responsible for the purchase and rebuilding of Beaumont House. Admiral Clarke CB DSO, a veteran of two world wars, had not missed a meeting in his five years of service, in spite of the long distance of his home from London.

Another serious loss, though not through death, was Sir Arthur Porritt, sergeant-surgeon to the Queen for fifteen years. He had been appointed Governor-General of New Zealand.

On a happier note (though not necessarily for the patient), was the admission again of Queen Elizabeth the Queen Mother. She was kept in, for an operation, from 10 December until after Christmas. She left, with many smiles and thanks, on 28 December.

'This year marks the end of an era,' reported Harold Wernher of 1967:

> It is the last full year of the Hospital at its present size. By the end of 1968 it is expected that the extension will be completed and the larger Hospital should be fully functioning by 1st January 1969, exactly seventy years after its foundation in 1899.

The noise of the building and demolition notwithstanding, three members of the Royal Family were admitted during the year; they were Princess Margaret, the Duchess of Kent and the Duke of Edinburgh.

The Appeals Office at Buckingham Place again had a difficult year. First Admiral Sir Alan Scott-Moncrieff was taken seriously ill, and was absent from his new office at Buckingham Place for much of the year. His Assistant Appeals Secretary, Peggy Phillips, and the other members of the staff had the extra burden of topping up the Extension

Appeal Fund and keeping pace with the unavoidable running expenses at a time of soaring inflation. For example, the old, high, rigid beds were no longer acceptable, especially as the new extension would be equipped with modern adjustable-height beds. The total cost was estimated at £4,500.

The year 1969, then, was to be another of these milestones in the life of King Edward VII's Hospital. Not only was it the seventieth anniversary of its founding by Sister Agnes, but Miss Agnes's successor (and near replica) Alice Saxby MVO was due to retire. Her place was to be taken by Miss Margaret Dalglish, one-time Deputy Matron of the Middlesex Hospital. It was arranged for Alice Saxby to have the rent-free use of a cottage in Cornwall, where her roots lay, the Council had been told, and where she was on intimate terms with the gentry and certain members of the aristocracy.

It would have been difficult to find a more inconvenient time for Miss Dalglish to take over. On the other hand, she was able to spend several months understudying Miss Saxby, for whom the changes were far more bewildering.

There were eight new appointments to the consultant staff to cope with the much increased accommodation, among them Dr Anthony Dawson, a Barts man, and future physician to the Queen. From St Thomas's Hospital came a surgeon whose surname had been associated with the early days of the Hospital; he was Hugh Lockhart-Mummery, son of the 'King Rectum' Lockhart-Mummery of the First World War.

There was another change in the Appeals Office when Admiral Sir Alan Scott-Moncrieff retired. He was succeeded by a 'flying man', Air Chief Marshal Sir Edmund Hudleston GCB, recently Air Aide-de-Camp to the Queen. He faced as tough a future as Margaret Dalglish.

CHAPTER 12

The Ongoing Struggle

THE LAST YEAR of the old decade coincided with the opening of a new era for the Hospital. More specifically, this began on 4 May 1969 when the much enlarged Hospital was formally re-opened after nine months of closure. The patients at once came pouring in as if a pied piper was playing in Beaumont Street, some in ambulances, others in taxis or private motor cars.

The Queen Mother herself was not far behind, this time as a visitor to her favourite Hospital. After her tour of the Hospital in its new guise, she became the guest of honour at a small gathering. Those present were members of the Council and several 'friends' of the Hospital who had contributed so generously to the cost of the extension and modernization, including Sir Isaac Wolfson and members of his family, and Mr and Mrs Cyril Kleinwort.

There were some losses in 1969 which were hard to bear. The resignation of Sir Reginald Macdonald-Buchanan was one. He had served as Chairman of both the House and Finance Committees since the opening in Beaumont Street, and was one of the early Trustees, stretching back in the Hospital's history to Sister Agnes's time. He continued to hold office as a Vice-President; and his son James was elected to the Council in his place, thus continuing the family connection. The Medical Committee also lost a valuable member with the retirement of Dr F. Campbell Golding. He was a veteran radiologist, and his final task was to advise on the setting up of an enlarged X-ray department.

But the worst blow sustained by the Hospital, perhaps the worst since Sister Agnes's death in 1941, was the retirement from the Council of Harold Wernher, whose family association with the Hospital went back to the very beginning. His own connection dated back more than forty years to the time when he became Deputy Chairman to Sister Agnes. 'Sir Harold's financial acumen, prudence and foresight, and his long experience of voluntary hospital work, have been of great value, and the Council is indebted to him also for his personal generosity.'

In his last address to the AGM, Wernher made characteristically frank reference to the ordeal (as indeed it had been) of the construction of the extension:

> I cannot pretend that the building of the extension has been free of anxieties, frustrations and setbacks. We were four months overdue in reopening the Hospital and there are still many loose ends to be completed. It may be six months before all evidence of building activity has ceased.

Admiral Sir David Luce, a noted submariner in the Second World War who subsequently rose to First Sea Lord, was appointed Chairman in Wernher's place.

Another loss through retirement was the Assistant Appeals Secretary, 'Peggy' Phillips. She had learned her skills from the best possible teacher, Sir Jameson Adams, and after his death worked with Admiral Sir Alan Scott-Moncrieff, and then Air Chief Marshal Sir Edmund Hudleston. Mrs N. Fillingham took her place at Buckingham Place.

At the AGM in 1970, the first presided over by Admiral Luce, he paid a deserved tribute to the medical and surgical staff:

> We express our warm thanks to the members of the Medical Committee and to the consultant staff for the outstanding services given to the Hospital, and without which we could not, of course, exist. I would also like to thank our consultants for many acts of generosity in waiving or reducing their fees to hard-up patients receiving help from the Samaritan Funds.

It was the first and last tribute the Admiral ever made as Chairman. Soon after, on 6 January 1971, he suddenly died, marking the shortest ever period in the office, and depriving the Hospital of a splendid man and admirable administrator.

As a stopgap, that retired old warhorse, Harold Wernher, occupied the Chairman's seat for the AGM on 30 March 1971. He was able to reassure the Council that Marshal of the RAF Sir Charles Elworthy had agreed to act as Chairman. This fine officer had recently retired as Chief of the Defence Staff, and was an old friend of the Hospital.

The Council over which he was to preside lost its Chief of Staff members, who were replaced by Admiral Sir Michael Pollock, General Sir Michael Carver and Air Chief Marshal Sir Denis Spotswood, an exceptionally charming man who had had a fine flying record in the Second World War, for which he was awarded a DSO and DFC.

Sir Ralph Marnham conceived the novel and admirable notion of organizing a meeting of the medical and surgical staff in order to exchange views on Hospital matters. It took place in the committee room at Agnes Keyser House. Not everyone could attend, but some useful work was done, and it was hoped this could become an annual event, as indeed it did.

Not long before this, the Hospital had had the concert pianist, Moura Lympany, as a patient. She was a friend of Brian Warren, the Hospital's surgeon–apothecary for so many years, who died as this book was being written. Just before Christmas 1970, he received a telephone call from a rather distraught Moura. She had just come from her doctor who confirmed what she feared, a cancer of the breast. Warren at once got into his car and drove round to the pianist's flat in Bruton Place, picked her up and without more ado drove her to Beaumont Street.

Moura Lympany had the required qualifications for registration, having many Army relations, and found herself in a single room on 23 December. Here one of the surgeons, Richard Handley OBE, examined her and told her that he would operate on 28 December. She went home for the intervening period before her biopsy, going to all the parties to which she had been invited in order to forget her troubles. Would she ever be able to play again?

When she came round Moura was relieved to hear that she did not have to endure chemotherapy. On the other hand, if she attempted to move her arm, 'I almost screamed with pain'. Surely, she thought, this was the end of her career. 'Sisters, doctors and all the staff were kindness itself. Matron [Dalglish] made a special point of seeing the New Year in with me, and we toasted each other and the wonderful hospital that was taking such wonderful care of me in champagne.'

But Moura's troubles were not yet over. A few days later she could not help brooding on her miserable situation, and she broke down and began to cry uncontrollably. 'I called a nurse and sobbed to her that I could not stop weeping. "Take a good slug of Scotch," she advised cheerfully. "And when you've drunk it, take another!"'

The advice was very much in the tradition of Sister Agnes.

Moura Lympany's arm, and her skills, recovered; she continued her wonderful career and was elevated to the Damehood in 1992.

In the summer HRH Princess Anne became a patient for the first time. At the other end of the social scale, this author was operated on by Rodney Sweetnam for a ruptured achilles tendon. This would not be worth mentioning except that a first evening experience introduced me to the spirit of the Hospital. Having smuggled in a bottle of sherry and a packet of small plastic mugs, I was about to take a first sip when the door swung open and in strode Matron Dalglish. Her welcoming smile turned to a shocked expression. 'Mr Hough,' Matron exclaimed, 'you know we do have schooners here for patients,' and sent for a tray of them.

The chief enemy of the Hospital, as for so many other voluntary institutions at the time, was soaring inflation, which affected food, wages . . . everything. Although inflation was, more or less, predictable, the second enemy was not. In December 1970 there had been a national power failure which lasted a week. Hospitals were given priority with the emergency supply, but the hazards and discomforts caused by this could not be ignored and the Council decided that a standby generator should be installed urgently. The cost was £13,500, an uncomfortably high figure, reduced by £1,000 by a gift from the Corporation of London.

In spite of this unforeseen expenditure, and an equally unexpected change in the financial law on Deeds of Covenant relating to charities, which would lead to a loss of approximately £16,000 per annum, the Hospital hoped to maintain the weekly cost of a bed at a basic £42 – actual cost £98. It was explained thus:

> The Accounts show that contributions from patients have risen by £14,000 during the year – mainly due to patients having increased their insurance against illness and allowing the Hospital to increase the charge for accommodation from the basic £42 to the actual cost of providing the bed on condition that this increase is covered by the patient's insurance. BUPA and PPP are aware of this procedure.

Thanks to the heroic work of the administrators and nursing staff, the number of patients admitted was a record 2,088. A high rate of bed occupancy was one of the most important contributions to sound finance. In 1972 it increased to 77.38 per cent from 75.54 per cent the previous year. One of the reasons why it was difficult to reach the target of 85 per cent–90 per cent was the practice of consultants and/or the patients' doctors of booking admission weeks in advance, and failing to cancel when not needed. The Council was determined to correct this anomaly, and did so.

Vere, Lady Birdwood, who had served the Hospital for twenty-five years, finally decided to retire. For all these years she had carried the ridiculously modest title of Secretary, when she really acted the role of Chief Administrator. She departed with peals of praise in her ears, and with the CVO awarded to her by HM the Queen in her Birthday Honours List. She was succeeded by Mr Kenneth Smith, a solicitor who had been Honorary Legal Adviser to the Hospital for many years. He was given the old and more appropriate title of House Governor. But it was by no means the end of Lady Birdwood's association with the Hospital. She agreed to serve on the Council, along with Dr Kenneth Milne, who unfortunately died later in the year.

A new name, and a very significant one for King Edward VII's, was HRH the Duke of Kent, who agreed to serve both on the Council and as a member of the Executive Committee. He also understood that when the Duke of Gloucester was no longer able to serve as President he would be asked to succeed him.

The report for the year 1973 was for the first time signed by

Kenneth Smith, and it contained some bleak news. The chief worry was the weight of essential expenditure, which seemed to pile up year by year to ever greater heights. A second X-ray room with fluoroscopic facilities was necessary, as it was becoming impracticable for patients to visit outside hospitals for this facility. The cost of the equipment alone was around £30,000. The modernization of three lifts was going to call for another £12,000. After acquiring a long lease on number 1 Beaumont Street to provide accommodation for the domestic and kitchen staff who were to lose their living quarters in Devonshire Close, provision had to be made for repairing and upgrading it. Another £30,000 would be the cost of that item.

Then there were two operating theatres on the fifth floor of the main building which required radical modernization. Initial verbal estimates for this delicate work were in the region of £100,000 and £200,000. Moreover, share prices had fallen over the year. The report read:

> This has not been a happy year for investments. However, Kleinwort, Benson [honorary financial consultants] have done their best to minimize the effect of falling share prices, and the Council wishes to thank them for all their help and advice.

This page of the history of King Edward VII's Hospital calls for a black funeral border in the old style of newspapers on the death of the sovereign, or the writing paper on the death of a relative. Following his retirement as Chairman of King Edward VII's Hospital, and the shedding of other major responsibilities, Harold Wernher began to show his age. Certainly, when this author met him at his Grosvenor Square flat in 1972, he looked aged and not very well. Unhappily, later in that year he fell ill and found himself in the Hospital, not in the chair at a meeting, which he always relished, but in bed. Cancer was diagnosed. He had not one, not two, but three serious operations and suffered much pain before he decided that he wanted to die at home. An ambulance took him to Luton Hoo, where he died on 30 June 1973, aged eighty.

> A memorial service was held at St Margaret's, Westminster. Lord Mountbatten gave the address, and spoke of his courage and modesty,

describing him as a 'fierce patriot' and recalling his contribution to Combined Operations during the war, so important to the success of the invasion of northern France. A letter from Gavin Astor in *The Times* was especially valued by Zia. He spoke of Harold as having been 'always ready to give time, help and advice to anyone who approached him, no matter how young or humble', of his 'well-informed mind' and his sense of humour, which 'cast a comfortable and relaxed atmosphere over any gathering – a business meeting, an annual staff dinner, a social occasion, a chat on the factory floor, a stroll with friends'.

After losing a Vice-President in 1973, the Hospital lost its President in the following year, Field Marshal and Marshal of the RAF HRH the Duke of Gloucester. The Duke had been particularly attached to King Edward VII's Hospital and his grandfather's close connection with it. During his long Presidency the Duke had been assiduous in his attention to his duties. Also, his kind paternalism would be much missed. The obvious candidate for taking his place was the Duke of Kent. The Queen, as Patron, approved, the Duke was willing to succeed his uncle, and approval of the Council was also forthcoming. The Duke has been in office ever since.

The leading figure in the list of retiring Council members was Lady Zia Wernher. Admirals Sir Peter Hill-Norton and Michael Pollock were two more to go. Their service replacements were Admiral Sir Edward Ashmore, General Sir Peter Hunt, and Air Chief Marshal Sir Andrew Humphrey.

The fight against inflation continued with a new ferocity during 1974. The Executive Committee was forced to raise fees for a private room from £63 a week to £98, an increase of 50 per cent in one year, in spite of sterling work by the Appeals Office led by Air Chief Marshal Sir Edmund Hudleston. Voluntary gifts totalled £118,196, which was £9,000 up on the previous year. In addition, two special appeals, one for the X-ray laboratory and the other for new operating theatres, raised £86,000 altogether.

There were other encouraging signs to cheer the Council. One of them was increased bed occupancy, up by 5 per cent to 84.24 per cent. But any further advance towards 90 per cent increased the risk of having to turn away emergency cases, a situation everyone was anxious to avoid: it was, after all, a sacred Sister Agnes principle, which had not dimmed more than thirty years after her death.

There was again great emphasis in the 1975 report of 'many head-aches due to the unremitting impact of inflation on all the Hospital's activities'. But it was the cost of nursing and domestic staff where the increase was most striking, this item alone having increased by £140,000 over the previous year. A further increase of fees was the inevitable consequence. From 1 July 1975 the cost to the patient in a private room went up again by almost 50 per cent, from £98 to £140 a week.

Mercifully, as before, when the financial and economic stresses increased in the outside world, the Appeals Office succeeded in wringing out of subscribers and supporters a significant increase in funds. There was an increase in the operating theatre special appeal from £47,000 at the end of 1974 to £175,000 twelve months later. 'In all,' ran the report, 'voluntary gifts received during the year amounted to nearly £234,000, £35,000 more than the Hospital has ever been given in any previous year.'

All this lightened the load of anxiety on the Executive Committee when work started on the replacement operating theatres which were badly needed if King Edward VII's Hospital was to continue to attract the very best surgeons.

The work with all its inevitable dust and disruption began in September 1975. Unlike the expansion exercise, the theatre-building proceeded without any delays; not much more than a year later the theatres were in full use and were much approved of by the consultants using them.

The Hospital was right up to date with all its facilities. This was in accordance with the traditions laid down by Sister Agnes, and set a shining example to all London hospitals. There was also another important factor, a political one. Since the very beginning of the National Health Service in 1947, there had grown up among some politicians a prejudice against and a suspicion of, any surviving private hospitals. If some scandal could have been exposed, revealing, say, inefficient nursing, a lack of adequate hygiene or failure of any of the facilities, it would be a gift for those intent on forcing the closure of all surviving private hospitals and nursing homes. There had been an unspoken awareness of this in Harold Wernher's time, and it had continued since.

The Executive Committee described 1977 as 'a year of consolidation', and this was a great relief for everyone concerned in the Hospital's running. Not that there was any diminution in activity, especially in Sir Edmund Hudleston's Appeals Office. He and his staff – Miss Pelly and Mrs Stevenson, and his volunteers Colonels W. McMilland, V. E. Scott-Bailey and H. F. Jackson – between them achieved a record sum of £218,000, which was £65,000 more than for any earlier year. As a result, fees did not have to rise, and there was a surplus of £39,000 for the year in the accounts.

But this same year of 1977 also saw the final link broken with the Wernher family. Four years after the death of her husband, Lady Zia Wernher died.

CHAPTER 13

New Works, New Faces

E ARLY IN 1977 Marshal of the RAF Lord Elworthy yielded the chairmanship of the Council to General Sir Peter Hunt GCB DSO OBE. Mark Baring remained Chairman of the Executive Committee, and Dr J. F. Dow Chairman of the Medical Committee.

Peter Hunt described 1978 as 'an encouraging year'. With justified satisfaction he continued:

> The number of patients the Hospital has treated, the correspondence received and the voluntary contributions received all show that present and future patients are anxious to be treated in a private hospital and that Sister Agnes's is high on their list of priorities because of its excellent reputation and comparatively low cost.

The bed occupancy, it was reported, had remained at about eighty per cent, but the cost of maintaining a bed also hit a new high of £287 a week, which led inevitably to another fee increase.

A new record was the figure raised by the Appeals Office, leading to a special vote of thanks to the Appeals Secretary, Air Chief Marshal Sir Edmund Hudleston.

But all this paled into insignificance with the news that an anonymous donor had agreed, through the trustees of his charitable trust, to a grant of no less than £750,000.

It was made clear that the money was for the express purpose of purchasing premises round the corner from Beaumont Street in Weymouth Street, then occupied by the Charterhouse Clinic.

Of the three-quarters of a million pounds, £300,000 would be spent on the purchase of the lease, and (an estimated) £200,000 on the conversion to the Hospital's requirements.

The remaining £250,000 is to match a similar sum from the Hospital, whose supporters would form an endowment fund especially for the benefit of this 'extension' so that the income from this fund will enable patients to be admitted there on the same terms as in Sister Agnes's. Thus the 'extension' will not be a financial burden on the existing Hospital.

By September 1978 the Hospital had raised over £175,000 of the quarter million, and consideration could be given to the use to which this unexpected bonus could best be put. The anonymous donor clearly wished that special consideration should be given to rheumatic and arthritic cases, which had been the speciality of the Charterhouse Clinic.

Plans were now drawn up for the construction in the basement of a physiotherapy department, complete with a hydrotherapy pool. Plans were drawn up for the ground floor which included a reception area and a pathological laboratory. The three floors above would accommodate twelve private rooms each giving a total maximum of three hundred and fifty patients a year. Staff quarters would be on the fourth floor.

The donor and his trustees compounded their generosity by making no further conditions, and were perfectly prepared, if the arrangement became a financial burden, for the Hospital to be free to sell the building, the proceeds accruing to the benefit of the Hospital.

It was as well that the donor and his trustees had been both generous and flexible, for almost at once the building next door to the Hospital, number 2 Beaumont Street, the premises of the National Heart Hospital, became available. This would be much more convenient than the Weymouth Street building. It was therefore decided that work would now start on a physiotherapy department and hydrotherapy pool in the basement of the main Hospital, where it remains to this day.

The Weymouth Street acquisition was to be used as a temporary home only for the pathology laboratory which would have to be moved while work in the basement was begun. The rest of Weymouth Street would be converted into staff bedrooms.

"These plans may appear complicated but the Executive Committee is confident that the end results will benefit the Hospital enormously.'

So the predicted period of tranquillity was not to be, and neighbours would for some time again live within the sound of hammers and saws and drills. This corner of Marylebone was like an intermittently active volcano, a mini Mount Etna, with dust lying like ash on the slopes or rising in clouds above the roofs of London W1.

The Samaritan Fund, set up to help indigent officers with their bed fees, received a generous and timely gift of £100,000 from Mr Reginald Graham. It was timely because it had once again become necessary to raise the fees, this time to £217 a week for a private room. The chief reason for this was an increase of some £100,000 in a full year in nurses' salaries, necessary to attract student recruits. A Government commission had awarded a 20 per cent increase in nurses' pay, on top of the usual annual increase.

A change of Matron is always an unwelcome event in a small private hospital. Before the arrival of Miss Margaret Dalglish, there had been only two Matrons, Sister Agnes herself and Miss Alice Saxby. In May 1980 Miss Dalglish reached retirement age, and it was announced that she would be succeeded by Miss Dorothy Shipsey, formerly Night Superintendent. The Council expressed its thanks to Miss Dalglish for her term of eleven years in office, as it did to Miss Anne Margerison, Miss Dalglish's deputy who was also due to retire. In the next Honours List the Queen bestowed the MVO on both women.

A further and equally regretted retirement in 1980 was that of Air Chief Marshal Sir Edmund Hudleston, whose tenure of office as Appeals Secretary was as arduous as it was successful. Hudleston was a remarkable man as this author can bear witness, having served under him during the closing months of the Second World War.

Hudleston's link with the Hospital was by no means severed, however, as he was elected a Council member the following year. In his place at the Appeals Office came Rear Admiral C. A. W. Weston CB.

Chairman Peter Hunt was able to report at the meeting on 1 February that the one-time Charterhouse Clinic had been made ready on time in 1981, with the pathology laboratory and lung function unit in full operation, and the rest of the building providing thirty bed-sitting rooms for nurses and domestic staff.

Even when the work was at its height at the ex-Charterhouse building, the functioning of the Hospital continued uninterrupted. The same could not be said of the underground work in Beaumont Street. The Chairman's report on the progress somewhat underplayed the mess and noise occasioned by this work:

> The building works in the basement of the Hospital have caused a considerable amount of inconvenience to patients and staff, but I am sure the new department will prove all this discomfort well worthwhile. The disturbance has also caused our bed-occupancy to drop during the last few months, and this lower bed-occupancy has resulted in the cost of maintaining a bed in Sister Agnes's rising substantially. However, it is hoped that the bed-occupancy figures will improve now that all rooms are back in commission.

The cost of building the subterranean pool and physiotherapy unit had been met from three sources: an anonymous donor, the King's Fund and the Queen Mother. The last of these was not direct. The Royal Warrant Holders' Association had arranged to present an eightieth birthday present to the Queen Mother, who, with the permission of the Association, diverted the sum of £83,500 direct to the Hospital. HM the Queen Mother became further associated with the pool and unit by declaring it open on 11 June 1981.

The previous October, the Council, presided over by HRH the Duke of Kent, met alone without any consultants for the first time for many years. At this meeting Admiral Sir Henry Leach, First Sea Lord and Chief of the Naval Staff, was welcomed as a new member, along with General Sir Edwin Bramall, Chief of the General Staff.

The early eighties proved as financially difficult as the previous decade. The bed fees rose with inflation, but few patients took advantage of the help offered by the Sister Agnes Benevolent Fund. It was clear that there was a reluctance to ask help from what was regarded by some officers, serving and retired, as charity. 'The Fund is capable of supporting more grants than we are at present receiving requests for,' ran the Chairman's report. As tactfully as possible, the idea of making a claim on this Fund was put about, especially to the elderly retired officers who were finding it difficult to keep up with the ever-increasing charges for private insurance.

There were several reasons why people who were connected with the Hospital, from volunteers in the Appeals Office to ward sisters and veteran members of the Council, were conscious of a change of 'feel' in Sister Agnes's in the early eighties. It was nothing to do with the fact of its growth, rather a sense of maturity. This was exemplified by the need to redecorate the outside of Agnes Keyser House, which to many minds and memories had only just been completed. Then, rewiring of the original Beaumont Street premises had an ageing feel about it – besides being costly and disruptive.

Nothing, however, pointed more sharply to the maturation of King Edward VII's Hospital for Officers than the celebrations associated with the eightieth anniversary, in May 1984, of the naming of the Hospital by the sovereign in 1904. With the Queen's gracious permission, a reception was held at St James's Palace hosted by the President, the Duke of Kent, and members of the Council. The report read:

> About 450 guests with working or historic connections with the Hospital were present. In addition to our President, we were honoured by the presence of her Royal Highness Princess Michael of Kent, Her Royal Highness Princess Alexandra the Hon. Mrs Angus Ogilvy, and the Hon. Angus Ogilvy. [The Duchess of Kent was unwell.] We are grateful to the Lord Chamberlain and his staff for their assistance in helping us to make this a happy and successful occasion.

To add to the historical element of this eightieth birthday, quite by chance a member of the Wernher family re-established the family on the Council. He was Nicholas Phillips, one of Harold and Zia's grandsons. Two notable Council members resigned at the same time, namely Air Chief Marshal Hudleston, who had also served so effectively as Appeals Secretary, and Major-General the Viscount

Monckton of Brenchley, who had served through the Second World War from beginning to end in the 5th Royal Inniskilling Dragoon Guards and the 3rd King's Own Hussars.

The rewirers began work in August 1984, and a fine old mess they made. Each ward in turn had to be closed for several months. In many places false ceilings had to be installed, and there were jokes about going back to gas lighting. However, all three wards were able to be reopened in March 1985. At the same time, as a first step towards conversion into all single rooms with private baths – the eventual ambition of the Executive Committee – the five-bedded ward on Ward 2 was converted into two single rooms, each with its own bathroom. This necessitated the running of a soil pipe right through the centre of the building. But there was sense behind this radical exercise, as every ward facing on to Beaumont Street could now be equipped with baths, when and if desired.

In the summer of 1985 the Hospital was composed of four main units: the heart, 5–10 Beaumont Street, which was the main Hospital building with its extension to the corner of Devonshire Street; 55–57 Beaumont Street, Agnes Keyser House, the nurses' home; 37A Devonshire Street, the senior nurses' home; and 56–60 Weymouth Street, once the Charterhouse Clinic and now the pathology and lung function laboratories, and residential rooms.

There must have been times when the Executive Committee cried out for modern purpose-built premises with plenty of space round it. Instead they resorted to the hopeful comment: 'When all the above work [rewiring and plumbing] has been completed the Hospital will be in first class condition and only routine maintenance should be required during the next few years.' 'We've heard all that before!' murmured Matron and the nurses!

Certainly, those responsible for the Hospital's accounts prayed that this would be the case. The audited accounts for the year ending 30 September 1984 revealed that the total expenditure was no less than £2,200,790. This figure, according to the Chairman, 'highlights the need to maintain the flow of income from all sources'.

Along at 6 Buckingham Place, the Appeals staff under the efficient Rear Admiral Charles Weston strove to maintain and then to exceed their previous figures. Fortunately, as the Chairman reported, 'the wealth of good will and benevolence directed towards the Hospital and its patients was remarkable'. He continued:

> Never have our benefactors been more generous, and the total sum of their efforts has resulted in the Hospital receiving voluntary gifts during the year totalling £702,266, an increase of £48,931 (7½ per cent) over the last year's total.

Proper credit was given to the staff of the Appeals Office for their achievements. This included the voluntary workers who gave their services, sometimes for years on end. One of them, Colonel Jackson, a distinguished former Commanding Officer in the Honourable Artillery Company, worked for seven years as a volunteer. He died, alas, in December 1984. Another volunteer, Colonel William McMillan, who died the following year, had put in thirteen years with scarcely a break.

For 1986 the Appeals Secretary was given separate and more generous space in the annual report. And for the first time Matron, Miss Dorothy Shipsey, was given a solus page for her report on that year.

Matron referred to the rewiring and decorating thus: 'Our patients were marvellous in their tolerance and understanding. At times it seemed like an assault course to get from one department to another!' There was abundant praise of her staff of ninety. 'I am constantly told both verbally and in letters that they are second to none, and the generosity from the patients to the Nurses' Christmas Fund reiterates their feelings and views.'

Of this total no fewer than sixty-three nurses attended outside lectures and study days. A number of the Hospital's consultants also gave up valuable time to give in-house lectures. Miss Shipsey treated her nurses with firmness and kindness in the real Sister Agnes style. She also knew that successful recruitment was the key to top quality in a nursing team. She conceived the idea of recruiting in Dublin. Nurses were trained to a high level in the Irish Republic. So she crossed the Irish Sea several times with her deputy, bringing with her photographs of the Hospital, and in particular of the nurses' accommodation. She placed advertisements in the Irish nursing magazines, giving the dates of her visit and inviting applications for interview. This proved highly successful at a time when the shortage of nurses in Britain was becoming serious. Miss Shipsey claims that she never approached a nursing agency after her method proved itself.

The year 1987 was notable, not for new wards or extensions, but for the new faces in the chair. The latest Chairman, Admiral of the Fleet Sir Henry Leach GCB, took over from General Sir Peter Hunt on 26 March. Leach had been a gunnery officer during the Second World War, at one time serving in the battleship *Duke of York*, in which he was involved in the successful action against the *Scharnhorst*; his father had gone down as Flag-Captain of the *Duke of York*'s sister ship, *The Prince of Wales*. Admiral Leach had been First Sea Lord and was already Chairman of St Dunstan's.

Another service appointment of great importance was that of Air Vice-Marshal Alfred Beill CB to replace Rear Admiral Weston as Appeals Officer. Weston, appointed in 1979, was thanked for 'his outstanding service to the Hospital' – and that was no overstatement. He would be much missed, as would Sir Henry Osmond-Clarke, who died that year. 'He was a very good and loyal friend of the Hospital whose interest in Sister Agnes's had continued ever since his appointment to the then newly created Consultants' list in 1951.' His widow bequeathed his surgical instruments to the Hospital.

Building works could not be entirely excluded from the consideration of the Council in spite of the 1984 commitment to 'only routine maintenance', and in the 1986 report attention was drawn to the imminent availability of number 2 Beaumont Street. When the leasehold became available it was seized upon by the Council – together with planning consent for demolition, which was marginally less expensive than the original plan to modify the existing building.

The estimated total cost was £3 million. Demolition was to start at the end of 1987. So once again the peace and quiet so desirable for any hospital was to be shattered, and once again Mount Etna would erupt in Marylebone.

The announcement of these works was followed by the inevitable notice, 'The Hospital will be launching a special appeal to help in financing the extension.' The one note of relief for neighbours (and patients and staff) was the statement, 'This will be the last practicable extension on the present site . . .'

Demolition work began in early May 1988, and the schedule for completion of the new building was the end of 1989. Unlike the earlier extension, the design was not intended to follow identically the main building, but to blend in comfortably with it, with floors on the same level.

Both Admiral Leach, as Chairman, and Air Vice-Marshal Beill as Appeals Secretary, attended their first meeting of the Council on 1 March 1988. Leach took the opportunity to open his report with his 'initial impressions' of the Hospital:

First, the efficient and unrelenting care for the patients – which I believe is what a hospital is all about. In all areas and at all levels there is evident a very fine spirit directed to this end. I see it as the main challenge to the Council to ensure that it never flags.

Second, the astonishing generosity – in time, in professional expertise and in money – displayed by so many towards Sister Agnes's. Without it that spirit to which I have just referred could not be the same.

And third, the dynamic atmosphere of the Hospital. The eager readiness to look ahead to the future and the resistance to comfortable reflections on the past or complacent satisfaction with the present.

It is therefore with feelings of pride, determination and confidence that I turn my pen to those other matters on which I think you would wish me to report.

This year, as always, there were the inevitable deaths to report, but in 1988 two were particularly poignant. Alice Saxby had died the previous November, forty-two years after Sister Agnes herself, upon whom Alice Saxby had modelled herself. Born in 1904, the year the Hospital was reborn as King Edward VII's Hospital, she lived to the age of eighty-three. Her death was widely noted. The *Daily Telegraph* obituary read:

Alice Saxby, who has died aged 83, was a meticulous Matron of King Edward VII's Hospital for Officers in Marylebone from 1948 to 1969: years in which the hospital expanded to accommodate such famous figures as Harold Macmillan and members of the Royal Family.

'Sax' was a neat, precise woman with soft light brown hair and a sharp wit; small in stature but tough. The soul of discretion and diplomacy, she was particularly close to the family of the Duke of Gloucester, and arranged the nursing of the last Duke (the hospital's president) at Barnwell after he suffered a stroke.

Sitting in her office by the front door of the hospital in Beaumont Street, accompanied by her little dog, the Matron knew everyone who came in and out. She paid punctilious attention to detail – characteristically ensuring that the hospital had an excellent chef when it reopened after the 1939–45 War – and was utterly dedicated to maintaining standards of care.

Alice Saxby trained at St Thomas's Hospital. During the 1939–45 War she took charge of the officers' villa known as the 'MLG' (from the days when it housed male low grade [less ill] patients) at the former mental institution Botley Park which became Thomas's Emergency Bed Service Hospital.

Although Miss Saxby played no active role in nursing politics, she was much concerned with the interests of her professional colleagues and had access to people of influence.

In retirement her former patients and colleagues continued to visit Sax, who had been appointed MVO.

Dorothy Shipsey, in her report, wrote:

It will come as sad news to you who have not already heard of the death of Miss Alice Saxby MVO, Matron from 1948 to 1969. She died peacefully at home in Maidenhead on 28th November. The respect, admiration and devotion shown to her by many friends, ex-patients, retired consultant staff and ex-nursing staff was highlighted by the large number who attended the Thanksgiving Service for her life which was held at St James's Church, Spanish Place, W1. All the Senior Members of the Royal Family were represented at the Service . . .

The other death, at the early age of seventy-one, was Sir Mark Baring KCVO on 6 February 1988. Although he knew Sister Saxby well, his committee work was less public than hers. His obituarist wrote:

Over thirty years ago he became a member of various planning sub-committees concerned with extensions and improvements to the

Hospital. In March 1951 he was elected to the House and Finance Committee and in 1969 Chairman of the Committee which in that same year became the Executive Committee as we know it today.

On his retirement as Chairman of the Executive Committee in 1986, he was made a Vice-President, an appointment which pleased us all and allowed us the continued benefit of his great knowledge of the Hospital.

CHAPTER 14

Centenary

As a further move to sustain morale among the nursing staff, Matron Shipsey introduced long-service badges, to be worn at all times when in uniform. For five years of service the badge was pale blue, for ten years deep red, and for twenty years the badge was of 9 carat gold and white enamel. The first presentation was on 20 October 1987. The Chairman of the Council, Sir Henry Leach, carried out the presentation, awarding two nurses ten-year badges and eight nurses pale blue five-year badges.

One year later, on 27 October 1988, the Council listened to the address given by HRH the Duke of Kent. He was concerned chiefly with congratulations, for it was a year of – once again – intense pressure on the Hospital's finances. There had been a rise in fees recently, but, he said, 'I am glad to learn that these fees have been kept down within the actual bed cost and what is of particular importance is that the fees for officer patients continue to be about one third of the full cost.'

He added, 'It is fairly common knowledge, too, that in the London area at present there are too many private beds chasing too few patients.'

A sadder note was struck by references to the deaths of two men who had given such fine service to the Hospital. Sir Mark Baring, recently retired as Chairman of the Executive Committee, had suffered a long illness; it was somewhat eased by treatment in the

Hospital to which he had given thirty years' service, but he died not long afterwards.

Sir Peter Hunt had been Chairman of the Council for nine years, 1978–87. 'He gained universal respect,' said the Duke, 'for his understanding, wisdom and straightforward approach to the many problems that the Hospital faced and overcame during those years. We remember him and his years in office with affection and much gratitude.'

Air Vice-Marshal Beill's report was mainly concerned with the special appeal for number 2 Beaumont Street. It was clearly going to be an uphill struggle to reach the target of £2 million. 'Alf' Beill decided that it would be appropriate, indeed necessary, to reintroduce fund-raising events to generate additional income. He was greatly assisted in this endeavour by Peter and Ann Hutley, who were very generous contributors to Sister Agnes's (i.e. Friends). Ann, the owner of the Wintershall Gallery, organized an art exhibition in Agnes Keyser House, the proceeds from which were sufficient to endow a room in number 2. A great deal more accrued from a pop concert at their Surrey estate; and, one way and another, this benevolent couple raised nearly £140,000 for the number 2 Building Fund.

Matron Dorothy Shipsey, too, had good news to report. She could even be crowned Queen of Recruitment, for she could proudly boast that, perhaps uniquely among London hospitals (and many outside London) and thanks largely to her visits to Ireland, the Hospital was fully staffed on day and night duty. Among her staff deserving special mention is the present Matron at the time of writing, Caroline Cassels, who was promoted in 1989 from Deputy Sister on Ward 3 to Senior Ward Sister on Ward 1.

A further cause for congratulation, again concerning Ward 1, was the completion of twenty-five years' service on this ward by Ines Olivera as a member of the domestic staff. Ines was a great character with an amazing memory for faces and an almost equal capacity for relying on the Spanish rather than the English language to communicate. Matron gave a small party in her honour at which she was presented with an engraved silver clock. It was one of the touches that kept the Hospital such a happy place.

Before attending the Council meeting on 23 October 1990, the Duke of Kent walked round the new extension, number 2, which had just been completed, to the relief of patients and staff – and neighbours, too.

The Duke pronounced himself impressed by the standard and quality of building and by its internal fittings and furnishings. 'It is my impression that there is a pleasant and efficient hospital environment at number 2 Beaumont Street. The staff have had a lot to put up with over the last two years,' he continued, by way of an apology, and then, almost in the same breath, he announced that the forthcoming complete refurbishment of the main Hospital building would, in effect, be just as hellish as the rebuilding of number 2.

Admiral Leach, as Chairman, then gave his report, opening with a tribute to Dorothy Shipsey on her completion of twenty-one years at the Hospital and ten years as Matron. He then recalled the formal opening of number 2 by the Queen and the Duke of Edinburgh. The total cost, including VAT and design team fees, had been £4.7 million.

This 'complete refurbishment' was not simply a question of a good clean and a lick of paint. It was more like, as one wag put it, 'Savoying the once-humble Sister Agnes'. Nor was it going to be cheap. In the words of Admiral Leach:

A contract has been entered into with Beazer Construction for the refurbishment of the main Hospital so that all patients' rooms will have en-suite bathrooms. The contract cost is £2,755,809, which with VAT and Design Team fees, will make a total cost of approximately £3,644,557.

Refurbishment was a term recently popularized by the American Ambassador to the Court of St James, Walter Annenberg, in connection with the radical improvements he ordered to be carried out at Winfield House, his residence in Regent's Park. It was certainly much used in Henry Leach's report because that was not the end of the reconstruction and redecoration of the Hospital in the years 1990–91. The one-time Charterhouse Clinic was to be altered to provide five additional rooms for the nursing staff; it was to have a new lift; and the pathology laboratory on the ground floor was to be 'refurbished', all at a cost of a further £375,000.

The final refurbishment for the year was of the kitchens on each floor of Agnes Keyser House, the nurses' home, which were to be refitted throughout.

Well over half a million pounds also had to be found for new equipment. The Hospital judged it essential for the latest equipment to be available, but it was increasingly and inevitably expensive. The new fluoroscopy unit alone cost £285,000.

With all this rebuilding and refurbishment, bed occupancy was seriously down, as the Chairman concluded in his report. Patients had to be turned away which meant valuable revenue lost in a very expensive year.

> With the smaller total number of beds in the 'new' Hospital (number 2) it will be vital that we have a high rate of bed occupancy. I should therefore be very grateful if all friends and supporters of the Hospital, and indeed everybody who reads this report, would do all they can to spread knowledge about the Hospital and the excellent facilities it offers.

In 1992 Brigadier Colin Harrisson, formerly of the Royal Green Jackets, took over at Sister Agnes's as House Governor. In 1995, following the retirement of Mr Robert Glossop as Chairman of the Executive Committee, it was decided to review the Hospital's top-level committee structure. This led to the establishment of a Management Board replacing the former Executive Committee. At the same time the House Governor assumed the new appointment of Chief Executive and became Chairman of the Management Board.

During his tenure as House Governor and now as Chief Executive, Brigadier Harrisson has successfully maintained the Hospital's position in the intensely competitive hospital market of the 1990s. His blend of firm leadership, humour and commitment to the ethos and future prosperity of the Hospital has welded the wide range of disciplines embraced by the Hospital's staff into a close-knit dedicated team.

It was noted by the Appeals Secretary in the 1992 report that

> the balance of £1.6 million from the Sorsbie legacies received during the year made a final total of some £8.25 million, a breathtaking figure, and

by a wide margin the biggest legacy ever received by the Hospital . . . In addition, some £660,000 was received from other bequests – a record for a single year.

Air Vice-Marshal Beill continued his rousing news: 'The charitable income for the year from donations, subscriptions and interest-free loans into the General Fund was £754,573 – another all-time record.'

Matron's report for the year was equally glowing with optimism, and of how 'delighted my staff and I are with the refurbishment of the Hospital. It is wonderful to have every room with a private bathroom while maintaining the individuality of each room.' Dorothy Shipsey concluded with congratulations to Sir Rodney Sweetnam, a pillar of the Hospital for so many years, on his KCVO, and to Mr John Dawson on his CVO.

This was all very reassuring, but both in the President's address and the Chairman's report there was a note of anxiety about the Hospital's future. The Duke of Kent spoke of the challenges of 1993. 'In these times of recession,' he said, 'it is vital that we seize any and every opportunity to market, albeit discreetly, what the Hospital has to offer amongst our potential patients.'

Finance and competition were the chief preoccupations of both the President and the Chairman. Private medicine had never been so competitive, with several new large and highly efficient hospitals springing up at the same time as the nation slid into deeper recession. At the same time, the negotiations with the private insurance companies, notably BUPA and PPP, were tough and unceasing. It was an aspect of running a private hospital that Sister Agnes never had to face, but if they had existed in her time, one can be sure that she would have treated them very roughly.

In the following year, wisely but reluctantly, the Executive Committee recommended inviting in a firm of management consultants.

Partly as a result of the management consultants' advice, 'some reorganization has inevitably taken place within the Hospital,' said the Duke of Kent in his address. 'Thirty posts within the Hospital were to go . . . mostly I am happy to say by natural wastage.'

The Duke also reflected that, at their last meeting, he was

looking ahead to a year in which the highest priorities would have to be attached to reducing our operating deficit, to improving our cost effectiveness and to marketing all that we have to offer at Sister Agnes's, against a background of fundamental change and fierce competition in the private sector, coupled with ever increasing pressure from the health insurance companies.

The emphasis in the Chairman's report was also on the finances of the Hospital, but Admiral Leach's conclusion was both admonitory and congratulatory – just the right mix for the difficult circumstances.

> I started by saying it had been an eventful year. This is the first time that such a fundamental review has been carried out in the Hospital. What we are doing is timely, prudent and healthy. It has by any standards been a turbulent and in some cases unsettling year for the staff. I continue to be immensely impressed by the manner in which they have reacted to the events of 1993 in a positive, resilient and efficient manner. In terms of patient care not one standard has been sacrificed, and I congratulate all our staff from top to bottom for the part they have played in this. Their commitment and professionalism will surely be needed as much in 1994 as it was in 1993.

As before, a positive note of cheer came from Air Vice-Marshal Alfred Beill. The charitable income from donations and subscriptions was up 14 per cent to £815,000, and the income from legacies up from £473,000 to £613,000.

In 1954 there had been twenty-eight names on the medical and surgical staff list. At that time Sister Agnes's was still a small hospital as it had been in Grosvenor Crescent. But forty years later it had grown into a medium-sized hospital with sixty-two beds, all of them en suite with a bathroom. The number of staff, cleaning, nursing and so on, had increased in proportion to about two hundred, as had the medical and surgical staff, which now numbered eighty-seven. Five of them were new this year, including John Scadding, the neurologist; the Emeritus Professor of Medicine in the University of London, Michael Shipley, the rheumatologist; and Wyndham Lloyd-Davies, the urologist and the head of clinical urology at St Thomas's Hospital.

In all the Hospital's history, as we have seen, the distinction associated with one's appointment as a consultant has never wavered, and has actually increased in line with the Hospital's standing as its centenary approaches. The King Edward VII's consultants have a unique role and status, and to 'join the club' requires not only competence and compatibility, but also the following of a procedure which is not a procedure at all but more like the indefinable method by which one lets it be known that if you were asked to join you might not refuse. Most of the more exclusive clubs operate on this same basis, and only those who are successful in their candidature fully understand the nuances of this odd but effective practice.

At the Council meeting on 8 November 1994, the Duke of Kent gave his customary address. This year he told the Council that he had spent much of the afternoon talking to members of the staff at all levels at their place of work and over a cup of tea. He continued:

> I have also been shown a large quantity of satisfaction surveys which have been completed by recent patients. These surveys speak for themselves. They reflect praise of the highest degree on all aspects of the Hospital, especially the standards of nursing care and the services provided by the clinical departments and the catering and domestic staffs . . . One is always struck by the inherently happy, helpful and caring atmosphere which meets you in all parts of the Hospital.

The Duke also made brief reference to the departure of Matron Shipsey earlier in May 1994. Dorothy ('Dot') Shipsey had been on the nursing staff for no fewer than twenty-five years, the last fourteen as Matron, a position of great responsibility. Her work had been praised to the skies, especially by the consultants.

A senior selection committee interviewed a number of candidates for Matron from inside the Hospital and elsewhere, and unanimously selected Miss Caroline Cassels, Senior Ward Sister of Ward 1, for the post. It was to prove to be a wise choice.

By the time of the annual Council meeting in November Matron Cassels was able to report:

Having already spent ten very happy years at King Edward VII Hospital for Officers, I was delighted to take up the post as Matron at the end of May.

While there have been some changes, the philosophy of the Hospital remains steadfastly unchanged, and one in which I believe whole-heartedly. The quality of nursing, too, continues to be consistently high, thanks to the hard work and loyalty of all the staff.

I look forward to the coming year, working with my team of dedicated nurses who continually strive to find ways of improving and developing the care which we provide for our patients.

Matron Cassels, when asked, 'Do you feel imbued with the spirit of Sister Agnes?' replies with an immediate and emphatic, 'Yes.' She felt that the whole Hospital, though unrecognizable to those who worked or were cared for at 17 Grosvenor Crescent, was infused with the soul and spirit of the founder who set up her first Hospital with her sister one hundred years ago.

Sister Agnes would certainly have been pleased and approving of the way the nurses of the 1990s are treated with such care, and generosity. Besides being paid above the Whitley Scale, their living accommodation in Agnes Keyser House is as good as a well-run hotel. Their food comes from the same kitchens as the patients' – see typical dinner menu in Appendix B. It is also freely available on their day off if required.

The nursing staff have a generous pension scheme and free private health care. They also have seven weeks of holiday a year and this can be taken to the individual nurse's convenience. Nurses from overseas, for example – there are a number from New Zealand, Australia and South Africa – tend to take all seven weeks without interruption, giving themselves a good break at home. Every hospital and nursing home in the land has recruitment problems from time to time. But Matron Cassels finds that most recruitment is carried out by word of mouth. Senior nursing staff are accommodated in self-contained flats in Horace Evans House round the corner in Devonshire Street.

The domestic staff and the cleaning are under the control of the Hotel Services Manager, Jeff Hoad, who has been in that post for many years. There is a strong measure of *esprit de corps* among the cleaning staff, too, who love their work and are well treated. Many are from abroad and remain loyal to the Hospital for years. Every year over the Christmas period when demands for beds greatly diminish, one of the three wards is closed down and subjected to a ferocious cleaning and painting. A stroll down one of the wards may cause visitors metaphorically to reach for their sunglasses, such is the gleaming cleanliness everywhere.

As the Hospital's centenary and the millennium both become imminent it is worth comparing Sister Agnes's today with conditions and circumstances fifty years earlier when Her late Majesty Queen Mary opened the reconstructured shell of a bombed nursing home in 1948.

Of the most striking points of contrast, the first is the competition between the surviving private hospitals in London. It is no exaggeration to say that it is cutthroat in its intensity, while at the same time the private health insurance companies have to be held at bay.

Related to this competition is the continual need to upgrade the equipment, at great cost, and keep pace with the 'state of the art' technology that continues to advance year by year. 'We've got to keep up!' is the repeated clarion call of the Hospital's Management Board.

In this struggle, Sister Agnes's enjoys two singular advantages. It is still governed by Royal Charter; and it has recently been granted accreditation by the King's Fund. This was only achieved after the most exhaustive and prolonged examination by officers of the Fund, the satisfactory completion of countless forms and the outcome of numerous inquiries. Accreditation is recognized in hospital terms as a sort of five-star diploma, or in restaurant terms, a triple Michelin rosette.

Other contrasts with 1948 are the brevity of patients' stays due to much quicker operating routines. This has its advantages but it adds to the administration costs. Another is the number of consultants. There are two main reasons why this has multiplied to around one hundred today. First, with the increasing degree of specialization within all branches of medicine, there is a need for more recently qualified consultants, as well as their maturer and more experienced colleagues. Second, because Sister Agnes's is effectively the Royal

Family's hospital, it requires the Household's medical staff to be on the list.

Unique is a dangerous word, but the Duke of Kent, when asked by this writer, 'What characterizes the Hospital that makes it unique?' replied without hesitation, 'The personal touch, the devotion of the nursing staff, and the feeling that it's like a family operation.'

This book has attempted to convey something of the spirit of Sister Agnes's, an indefinable mixture of caring, efficiency and happiness which is indeed unique.

APPENDIX A

Past and Present Holders of Office

President

1904–35	HRH The Prince of Wales
1936–74	HRH The Duke of Gloucester
1975–	HRH The Duke of Kent

Chairman of Council

1930–69	Major General Sir Harold Wernher Bt. GCVO
1969–71	Admiral Sir David Luce GCB DSO OBE
1971–78	Marshal of the Royal Air Force Lord Elworthy GCB CBE DSO LVO DFC AFC
1978–87	General Sir Peter Hunt GCB DSO OBE DL
1987–98	Admiral of the Fleet Sir Henry Leach GCB DL
1998–	Marshal of the Royal Air Force Lord Craig GCB OBE

Chairman of Management Board
(*formerly House & Finance Committee and later Executive Committee*)

1931–39	Sister Agnes
1940–47	Major General Sir Harold Wernher Bt. GCVO
1948–68	Sir Reginald Macdonald-Buchanan
1969–86	Sir Mark Baring KCVO
1986–92	Mr Keith E. Wright
1992–95	Mr Robert Glossop
1995–96	Mr Miles Rivett-Carnac
1996–	Brigadier C. J. M. Harrisson OBE

Chief Executive
(*formerly House Governor*)

1938–50	Sir George Ogilvie KCIE CSI
1950–72	Vere, Lady Birdwood CVO

1972–85	Mr K. B. Smith CVO
1985–92	Commander I. K. Brooks OBE RN
1992–	Brigadier C. J. M. Harrisson OBE

Matron

1899–1940	Sister Agnes
(Hospital closed from September 1940 to October 1948)	
1948–69	Miss Alice Saxby MVO
1969–80	Miss Margaret Dalglish MVO
1980–94	Miss Dorothy Shipsey MVO (now Countess Cadogan)
1994–	Miss Caroline Cassels

Director of Marketing and Fund-raising
(formerly Appeals Secretary)

1949–62	Commander Sir Jameson Adams KCVO CBE DSO RNR
1962–68	Admiral Sir Alan Scott Moncrieff KCB CBE DSO DL
1968–79	Air Chief Marshal Sir Edmund Hudleston GCB CBE
1979–87	Rear Admiral C. A. W. Weston CB
1987–96	Air Vice-Marshal A. Beill CB
1996–8	Mrs Anne Fragniere
1998–	Mr Tim Law

A Typical Dinner Menu

King Edward VII's

HOSPITAL FOR OFFICERS

Dinner

Starters

Cream of Carrot and Basil Soup

Deep Fried Pate Stuffed Mushrooms

Main Courses

Grilled Breast of Duck in Red Wine Sauce

Salmon Roulade with Noir

Vulsome Salad

Served with Delmonico Macaire potatoes and a selection of
seasonal vegetables

Puddings

Poached Pears in Red Wine and Caramel Sauce

Jamaican Rum and Raisin Ice Cream

Mango Sorbet with Grand Marnier

Fresh Fruit

Cheese Plate

Cherrywood Dolcelatte Port Salut

Please choose your wine order from the Wine List

Sources

All unattributed quotations are from the Hospital archives and from contributions by patients and officers of Sister Agnes's who kindly wrote in response to appeals from the Hospital and from the Press. Other published sources are as follows:

Chapter 1
1 Hough, R., *Edward and Alexandra* (1982), p. 188.
2 St Aubyn, G., *Edward VII: Prince and King* (1979), p. 378.
3 Pakenham, T., *The Boer War* (1979), paperback edn, p. 237.

Chapter 2
1 Magnus, P., *King Edward VII* (1964), paperback edn, p. 335.
2 *London Gazette*, 9 August 1901, no. 27344, p. 5256.

Chapter 3
1 St Aubyn, op. cit., p. 407.
2 Cortissoz, F., *Life of Whitelaw Reid*, vol. ii (1921), p. 144.
3 Royal Archives, G V AA 55.
4 Lee, S., *King Edward VII*, vol. ii (1926), p. 722.
5 Ibid.
6 Royal Archives, K G V Diary, February 27 1911.
7 Rose, K., *King George V* (1983), p. 166.
8 Thomson, G. M., *The Twelve Days* (1964), pp. 17–18.

Chapter 4
1 Churchill, W. S., *The World Crisis*, vol. i (1923), p. 197.
2 Falls, C., *The First World War* (1960), p. 16.
3 Buchan, J., *Francis and Riversdale Grenfell* (1920), pp. 197–8.

Chapter 5
1 Falls, op. cit., p. 63.
2 Churchill, op. cit., p. 467.

3 Hough, op. cit., p. 334.
4 Read, L., *1915* (1993), p. 71.
5 Ibid., p. 350.
6 Ibid., p. 359.
7 Ibid., p. 450.

Chapter 6
1 Rose, op. cit., p. 400.
2 Ibid., p. 401.

Chapter 8
1 Nicolson, N. (ed.), *Diaries and Letters of Harold Nicolson* (1966), p. 322.
2 Ibid., p. 331.
3 Ibid.
4 Churchill, W. S., *The Second World War*, vol. i (1948), p. 320.
5 Royal Archives, PP G VI 5264.
6 Churchill, op. cit., vol. ii (1949), p. 303.
7 Official report.
8 Royal Archives, G VI PS 725.
9 Royal Archives, G V cc 47.

Chapter 9
1 Trevelyan, R., *Grand Dukes and Diamonds* (1991), p. 352

Chapter 10
1 Longford, E., *Elizabeth R* (1983), p. 143.
2 Avon, Earl of, *The Memoirs of Sir Anthony Eden: Full Circle* (1960), p. 40.

Chapter 11
1 Churchill, W. S., *His Father's Son* (1996), p. 448.
2 Davie, M. (ed.), *The Diaries of Evelyn Waugh* (1976), p. 792.

Index